Richard Doddridge Blackmore

Mary Anerley, a Yorkshire Tale

Vol.1

Richard Doddridge Blackmore

Mary Anerley, a Yorkshire Tale
Vol.1

ISBN/EAN: 9783337024314

Printed in Europe, USA, Canada, Australia, Japan

Cover: Foto ©Andreas Hilbeck / pixelio.de

More available books at **www.hansebooks.com**

MARY ANERLEY.

VOL. I.

LONDON :
GILBERT AND RIVINGTON, PRINTERS,
ST. JOHN'S SQUARE.

MARY ANERLEY.

A YORKSHIRE TALE.

BY

R.ᵈ D.ʳ BLACKMORE,

AUTHOR OF "ALICE LORRAINE," ETC.

ὦ ξεῖνοι, τίνες ἐστέ; πόθεν πλεῖθ᾽ ὑγρὰ κέλευθα;
ἤ τι κατὰ πρῆξιν, ἢ μαψιδίως ἀλάλησθε,
οἷά τε ληϊστῆρες ὑπεὶρ ἅλα, τοί τ᾽ ἀλόωνται,
ψυχὰς παρθέμενοι, κακὸν ἀλλοδαποῖσι φέροντες;
Od. iii. 71.

IN THREE VOLUMES.

VOL. I.

London:

SAMPSON LOW, MARSTON, SEARLE, & RIVINGTON,

CROWN BUILDINGS, 188, FLEET STREET.

1880.

TO MY OLD AND VALUED FRIEND,

ARTHUR JOSEPH MUNBY, M.A., F.S.A.,

OF LINCOLN'S INN, BARRISTER-AT-LAW,

AND OF CLIFTON HOLME, NEAR YORK,

This Book,

OWING MUCH TO HIS KIND AID, IS

GRATEFULLY DEDICATED.

CONTENTS.

MARY ANERLEY.

CHAPTER I.

HEADSTRONG AND HEADLONG.

FAR from any house, or hut, in the depth of dreary moorland, a road, unfenced and almost unformed, descends to a rapid river. The crossing is called the " Seven Corpse Ford," because a large party of farmers, riding homeward from Middleton, banded together and perhaps well-primed through fear of a famous highwayman, came down to this place on a foggy evening, after heavy rainfall. One of the company set before them what the power of the water was, but they laughed at him and spurred into it, and one alone spurred out of it. Whether taken with fright, or with too much courage, they laid hold of one another,

and seven out of eight of them, all large
farmers, and thoroughly understanding land,
came never upon it alive again ; and their
bodies, being found upon the ridge that cast
them up, gave a dismal name to a place that
never was merry in the best of weather.

However, worse things than this had happened ; and the country is not chary of its
living, though apt to be scared of its dead ;
and so the ford came into use again, with a
little attempt at improvement. For those
farmers being beyond recall, and their families
hard to provide for, Richard Yordas of Scargate Hall, the chief owner of the neighbourhood, set a long heavy stone up on either
brink, and stretched a strong chain between
them ; not only to mark out the course of
the shallow, whose shelf is askew to the chan-
nel, but also that any one being washed away
might fetch up, and feel how to save himself.
For the Tees is a violent water sometimes,
and the safest way to cross it is to go on till
you come to a good stone bridge.

Now forty years after that sad destruction
of brave but not well-guided men, and thirty
years after the chain was fixed, that their
sons might not go after them, another thing

happened at "Seven Corpse Ford," worse
than the drowning of the farmers. Or, at any
rate, it made more stir (which is of wider
spread than sorrow) because of the eminence
of the man, and the length and width of his
property. Neither could any one at first
believe in so quiet an end to so turbulent a
course. Nevertheless it came to pass, as
lightly as if he were a reed or a bubble of
the river that belonged to him.

It was upon a gentle evening, a few days
after Michaelmas of 1777. No flood was in
the river then, and no fog on the moorland,
only the usual course of time, keeping the
silent company of stars. The young moon
was down, and the hover of the sky (in doubt
of various lights) was gone, and the equal
spread of obscurity soothed the eyes of any
reasonable man.

But the man who rode down to the river
that night had little love of reason. Headstrong chief of a headlong race, no will must
depart a hair's breadth from his; and fifty
years of arrogant port had stiffened a neck
too stiff at birth. Even now in the dim light
his large square form stood out against the
sky, like a cromlech, and his heavy arms

swung like gnarled boughs of oak, for a
storm of wrath was moving him. In his
youth he had rebelled against his father;
and now his own son was a rebel to
him.

"Good, my boy, good!" he said within his
grizzled beard, while his eyes shone with fire,
like the flints beneath his horse; "you have
had your own way, have you, then? But
never shall you step upon an acre of your
own; and your timber shall be the gallows.
Done, my boy, once and for ever."

Philip, the squire, the son of Richard, and
father of Duncan Yordas, with fierce satisfaction struck the bosom of his heavy Brad-
ford riding-coat, and the crackle of parchment
replied to the blow, while with the other hand
he drew rein on the brink of Tees sliding
rapidly.

The water was dark with the twinkle of
stars, and wide with the vapour of the valley;
but Philip Yordas in the rage of triumph
laughed and spurred his reflecting horse.

"Fool!" he cried without an oath—no
Yordas ever used an oath, except in playful
moments—"fool! what fear you? There
hangs my respected father's chain. Ah, he

was something like a man! Had I ever
dared to flout him so, he would have hanged·
me with it."

Wild with his wrong, he struck the rowel
deep into the flank of his wading horse, and
in scorn of the depth drove him up the river.
The shoulders of the swimming horse broke
the swirling water, as he panted and snorted
against it; and if Philip Yordas had drawn
back at once, he might even now have crossed
safely. But the fury of his blood was up,
the stronger the torrent the fiercer his will,
and the fight between passion and power
went on. The poor horse was fain to swerve
back at last; but he struck him on the head
with a carabine, and shouted to the torrent,—

"Drown me, if you can. My father used
to say that I was never born to drown. My
own water drown me! That would be a
little too much insolence."

"Too much insolence" were his last words.
The strength of the horse was exhausted.
The beat of his legs grew short and faint,
the white of his eyes rolled piteously, and the
gurgle of his breath subsided. His heavy
head dropped under water, and his sodden
crest rolled over, like seaweed where a wave

breaks. The stream had him all at its mercy, and showed no more than his savage master · had, but swept him a wallowing lump away, ·and over the reef of the crossing. With both feet locked in the twisted stirrups, and right arm broken at the elbow, the rider was swung (like the mast of a wreck) and flung with his head upon his father's chain. There he was held by his great square chin—for the jar of his backbone stunned him—and the weight of the swept-away horse broke the neck which never had known how to bend. In the morning a peasant found him there, not drowned but hanged, with eyes wide open, a swaying corpse upon a creaking chain. So his father (though long in the grave) was his death, as he often had promised to be to him; while he (with the habit of his race) clutched fast with dead hand on dead bosom, the instrument securing the starvation of his son.

Of the Yordas family truly was it said, that the will of God was nothing to their will —as long as the latter lasted—and that every man of them scorned all Testament, old or new, except his own.

CHAPTER II.

SCARGATE HALL.

NEARLY twenty-four years had passed since
Philip Yordas was carried to his last (as well
as his first) repose, and Scargate Hall had
enjoyed some rest from the turbulence of
owners. For as soon as Duncan (Philip's son,
whose marriage had maddened his father)
was clearly apprised by the late squire's
lawyer of his disinheritance, he collected his
own little money and his wife's, and set sail
for India. His mother, a Scotchwoman of
good birth, but evil fortunes, had left him
something; and his bride (the daughter of
his father's greatest foe) was not altogether
empty-handed. His sisters were forbidden
by the will to help him with a single penny;
and Philippa, the elder, declaring and believing that Duncan had killed her father,

strictly obeyed the injunction. But Eliza, being of a softer kind, and herself then in love with Captain Carnaby, would gladly have aided her only brother, but for his stern refusal. In such a case, a more gentle nature than ever endowed a Yordas might have grown hardened and bitter; and Duncan, being of true Yordas fibre (thickened and toughened with slower Scotch sap) was not of the sort to be ousted lightly, and grow at the feet of his supplanters.

Therefore he cast himself on the winds, in search of fairer soil, and was not heard of in his native land; and Scargate Hall and estates were held by the sisters in joint-tenancy, with remainder to the first son born of whichever it might be of them. And this was so worded through the hurry of their father to get some one established in the place of his own son.

But from paltry passions, turn away a little while to the things which excite, but are not excited by them.

Scargate Hall stands, high and old, in the wildest and most rugged part of the wild and rough North Riding. Many are the tales about it, in the few and humble cots, scattered in the modest distance, mainly to look

up at it. In spring and summer, of the years
that have any, the height and the air are not
only fine, but even fair and pleasant. So do
the shadows and the sunshine wander, elbow-
ing into one another on the moor, and so does
the glance of smiling foliage soothe the aus-
terity of crag and scaur. At such time also,
the restless torrent (whose fury has driven
content away through many a short day and
long night) is not in such desperate hurry to
bury its troubles in the breast of Tees, but
spreads them in language that sparkles to the
sun, or even makes leisure to turn into corners
of deep brown study about the people on its
banks—especially perhaps the miller.

But never had this impetuous water more
reason to stop and reflect upon people of
greater importance, who called it their own,
than now when it was at the lowest of itself,
in August of the year 1801.

From time beyond date the race of Yordas
had owned and inhabited this old place. From
them the river, and the river's valley, and the
mountain of its birth took name, or else perhaps gave name to them; for the history of
the giant Yordas still remains to be written,
and the materials are scanty. His present

descendants did not care an old song for his
memory, even if he ever had existence to
produce it.   Piety (whether in the Latin sense
or English) never had marked them for her
own; their days were long in the land, through
a long inactivity of the Decalogue.

And yet in some manner this lawless race
had been as a law to itself throughout.   From
age to age came certain gifts and certain ways
of management, which saved the family life
from falling out of rank and land and lot.
From deadly feuds, exhausting suits, and
ruinous profusion, when all appeared lost,
there had always arisen a man of direct lineal
stock, to retrieve the estates and reprieve the
name.   And what is still more conducive to
the longevity of families, no member had
appeared as yet of a power too large and an
aim too lofty, whose eminence must be cut
short with axe, outlawry, and attainder.
Therefore there ever had been a Yordas, good
or bad (and by his own showing more often of
the latter kind), to stand before heaven, and
hold the land, and harass them that dwelt
thereon.   But now at last the world seemed
to be threatened with the extinction of a fine
old name.

When Squire Philip died in the river, as above recorded, his death, from one point of view, was dry, since nobody shed a tear for him, unless it was his child Eliza. Still he was missed and lamented in speech, and even in eloquent speeches, having been a very strong Justice of the Peace, as well as the foremost of riotous gentlemen keeping the order of the county. He stood above them in his firm resolve to have his own way always, and his way was so crooked that the difficulty was to get out of it and let him have it. And when he was dead, it was either too good or too bad to believe in; and even after he was buried it was held that this might be only another of his tricks.

But after his ghost had been seen repeatedly, sitting on the chain and swearing, it began to be known that he was gone indeed, and the relief afforded by his absence endeared him to sad memory. Moreover his good successors enhanced the relish of scandal about him, by seeming themselves to be always so dry, distant, and unimpeachable. Especially so did " My Lady Philippa," as the elder daughter was called by all the tenants and dependents, though the family now held no title of honour.

Mistress Yordas, as she was more correctly styled by usage of the period, was a maiden lady of fine presence, uncumbered as yet by weight of years, and only dignified thereby. Stately, and straight, and substantial of figure, firm but not coarse of feature, she had reached her forty-fifth year without an ailment or a wrinkle. Her eyes were steadfast, clear, and bright, well able to second her distinct calm voice, and handsome still, though their deep blue had waned into a quiet, impenetrable grey; while her broad clear forehead, straight nose, and red lips might well be considered as comely as ever, at least by those who loved her. Of these, however, there were not many; and she was content to have it so.

Mrs. Carnaby, the younger sister, would not have been content to have it so. Though not of the weak lot which is enfeoffed to popularity, she liked to be regarded kindly, and would rather win a smile than exact a curtsey. Continually it was said of her that she was no genuine Yordas, though really she had all the pride, and all the stubbornness of that race, enlarged perhaps, but little weakened, by

severe afflictions. This lady had lost a be-
loved husband, Colonel Carnaby, killed in
battle; and after that four children of the five
she had been so proud of. And the waters
of affliction had not turned to bitterness in
her soul.

Concerning the outward part—which matters more than the inward, at first hand—
Mrs. Carnaby had no reason to complain of
fortune. She had started well as a very fine
baby, and grown up well into a lovely maiden,
passing through wedlock into a sightly matron,
gentle, fair, and showing reason. For generations it had come to pass that those of the
Yordas race who deserved to be cut off for
their doings out of doors were followed by
ladies of decorum, self-restraint, and regard
for their neighbour's landmark. And so it
was now with these two ladies, the handsome
Philippa and the fair Eliza leading a peaceful
and reputable life, and carefully studying their
rent-roll.

It was not, however, in the fitness of things
that quiet should reign at Scargate Hall for a
quarter of a century; and one strong element
of disturbance grew already manifest. Under
the will of Squire Philip the heir apparent

was the one surviving child of Mrs. Carnaby.

If ever a mortal life was saved by dint of sleepless care, warm coddling, and perpetual doctoring, it was the precious life of Master Lancelot Yordas Carnaby. In him all the mischief of his race revived, without the strong substance to carry it off. Though his parents were healthy and vigorous, he was of weakly constitution, which would not have been half so dangerous to him, if his mind also had been weakly. But his mind (or at any rate that rudiment thereof which appears in the shape of self-will even before the teeth appear) was a piece of muscular contortion, tough as oak, and hard as iron. "Pet" was his name with his mother and his aunt; and his enemies (being the rest of mankind) said that pet was his name and his nature.

For this dear child could brook no denial, no slow submission to his wishes; whatever he wanted must come in a moment, punctual as an echo. In him reappeared not the stubbornness only, but also the keen ingenuity of Yordas in finding out the very thing that never should be done, and then the unerring perception of the way in which it could be

done most noxiously. Yet any one looking
at his eyes would think how tender and bright
must his nature be! "He favoureth his fore-
elders; how can he help it?" kind people
exclaimed, when they knew him. And the
servants of the house excused themselves
when condemned for putting up with him,
"Naa, ye dawn't knaw t' yoong Maaster.
He's that fratchy and auld-farrand he mun
gau' 's own gaat, if ye weän't chawk him."

Being too valuable to be choked, he got
his own way always.

CHAPTER III.

A DISAPPOINTING APPOINTMENT.

For the sake of Pet Carnaby and of themselves, the ladies of the house were disquieted now, in the first summer weather of a changeful year, the year of our Lord 1801. And their trouble arose as follows :—

There had long been a question between the sisters and Sir Walter Carnaby, brother of the late colonel, about an exchange of outlying land, which would have to be ratified by "Pet" hereafter. Terms being settled and agreement signed, the lawyers fell to at the linked sweetness of deducing title. The abstract of the Yordas title was nearly as big as the parish Bible, so in and out had their dealings been, and so intricate their pugnacity.

Among the many other of the Yordas freaks was a fatuous and generally fatal one. For the slightest miscarriage they discharged their lawyer, and leaped into the office of a new one! Has any man moved in the affairs of men, with a grain of common sense, or half a penny-weight of experience, without being taught that an old tenter-hook sits easier to him than a new one? And not only that, but in shifting his quarters he may leave some truly fundamental thing behind.

Old Mr. Jellicorse, of Middleton in Teesdale, had won golden opinions everywhere. He was an uncommonly honest lawyer, highly incapable of almost any trick, and lofty in his view of things, when his side of them was the legal one. He had a large collection of those interesting boxes which are to a lawyer and his family better than caskets of silver and gold; and especially were his shelves furnished with what might be called the library of the Scargate title-deeds. He had been proud to take charge of these nearly thirty years ago, and had married on the strength of them, though warned by the rival from whom they were wrested that he must not hope to keep them long. However, through the peaceful incumbency of ladies, they remained in his office all those years.

This was the gentleman who had drawn
and legally sped to its purport the will of the
lamented Squire Philip; who refused very
clearly to leave it, and took horse to flourish
it at his rebellious son. Mr. Jellicorse
had done the utmost, as behoved him,
against that rancorous testament; but meeting with silence more savage than words,
and a bow to depart, he had yielded; and
the Squire stamped about the room until his
job was finished.

A fact accomplished, whether good or bad,
improves in character with every revolution
of this little world around the sun, that
heavenly example of subservience. And now
Mr. Jellicorse was well convinced, as nothing
had occurred to disturb that will, and the life
of the testator had been sacrificed to it, and
the devisees under it were his own good
clients, and some of his finest turns of words
were in it, and the preparation, execution,
and attestation, in an hour and ten minutes
of the office clock, had never been equalled
in Yorkshire before, and perhaps never
honestly in London—taking all these things
into conscious or unconscious balance, Mr.
Jellicorse grew into the clear conviction that

"righteous and wise" were the words to be used whenever this will was spoken of.

With pleasant remembrance of the starveling fees wherewith he used to charge the public, ere ever his golden spurs were won, the prosperous lawyer now began to run his eye through a duplicate of an abstract furnished upon some little sale about forty years before. This would form the basis of the abstract now to be furnished to Sir Walter Carnaby, with little to be added but the will of Philip Yordas, and statement of facts to be verified. Mr. Jellicorse was fat, but very active still; he liked good living, but he liked to earn it, and could not sit down to his dinner without feeling that he had helped the Lord to provide these mercies. He carried a pencil on his chain, and liked to use it ere ever he began with knife and fork. For the young men in the office, as he always said, knew nothing.

The day was very bright and clear, and the sun shone through soft lilac leaves on more important folios, while Mr. Jellicorse, with happy sniffs—for his dinner was roasting in the distance—drew a single line here, or a double line there, or a gable on the margin

of the paper, to show his head clerk what to
cite, and in what letters, and what to omit,
in the abstract to be rendered. For the good
solicitor had spent some time in the chambers
of a famous conveyancer in London, and
prided himself upon deducing title, directly,
exhaustively, and yet tersely, in one word,
scientifically, and not as the mere quill-driver.
The title to the hereditaments, now to be
given in exchange, went back for many generations; but as the deeds were not to pass,
Mr. Jellicorse, like an honest man, drew a
line across, and made a star at one quite old
enough to begin with, in which the little
moorland farm in treaty now was specified.
With hum and ha of satisfaction he came
down the records, as far as the settlement
made upon the marriage of Richard Yordas
of Scargate Hall, Esquire, and Eleanor, the
daughter of Sir Fursan de Roos. This document created no entail, for strict settlements
had never been the manner of the race; but
the property assured in trust, to satisfy the
jointure, was then declared subject to joint and
surviving powers of appointment limited to
the issue of the marriage, with remainder to
the uses of the will of the aforesaid Richard

Yordas, or, failing such will, to his right heirs for ever.

All this was usual enough, and Mr. Jellicorse heeded it little, having never heard of any appointment, and knowing that Richard, the grandfather of his clients, had died, as became a true Yordas, in a fit of fury with a poor tenant, intestate, as well as unrepentant. The lawyer, being a slightly pious man, afforded a little sigh to this remembrance, and lifted his finger to turn the leaf, but the leaf stuck a moment, and the paper being raised at the very best angle to the sun he saw, or seemed to see, a faint red line, just over against that appointment clause. And then the yellow margin showed some faint red marks.

" Well, I never—" Mr. Jellicorse exclaimed, " certainly never saw these marks before. Diana, where are my glasses ?"

Mrs. Jellicorse had been to see the potatoes on (for the new cook simply made " kettlefuls of fish" of everything put upon the fire), and now at her husband's call she went to her work-box for his spectacles, which he was not allowed to wear except on Sundays, for fear of injuring his eyesight. Equipped with

these, and drawing nearer to the window, the
lawyer gradually made out this—first a broad
faint line of red, as if some attorney, now a
ghost, had cut his finger, and over against
that in small round hand the letters " v. b. c."
Mr. Jellicorse could swear that they were
"v. b. c."

" Don't ask me to eat any dinner to-day,"
he exclaimed, when his wife came to fetch him.
" Diana, I am occupied; go and eat it up
without me."

" Nonsense, James," she answered calmly;
" you never get any clever thoughts by
starving."

Moved by this reasoning, he submitted, fed
his wife and children, and own good self, and
then brought up a bottle of old Spanish wine,
to strengthen the founts of discovery. Whose
writing was that upon the broad marge of ver-
bosity ? Why had it never been observed before ? Above all, what was meant by "v. b. c."?

Unaided, he might have gone on for ever,
to the bottom of a butt of Xeres wine; but
finding the second glass better than the first,
he called to Mrs. Jellicorse, who was in the
garden gathering striped roses, to come and
have a sip with him, and taste the yellow

cherries. And when she came promptly with
the flowers in her hand, and their youngest
little daughter making sly eyes at the fruit,
bothered as he was, he could not help smiling
and saying, " Oh! Diana, what is ' v. b. c.' ?"

" Very black currants, papa!" cried Emily,
dancing a long bunch in the air.

" Hush, dear child, you are getting too forward," said her mother, though proud of her
quickness. " James, how should I know what
' v. b. c.' is? But I wish most heartily that -
you would rid me of my old enemy, box C. I
want to put a hanging-press in that corner,
instead of which you turn the very passages
into office."

" Box C? I remember no box C."

" You may not have noticed the letter C
upon it, but the box you must know as well
as I do. It belongs to those proud Yordas
people, who hold their heads so high, forsooth,
as if nobody but themselves belonged to a
good old county family! That makes me
hate the box the more."

" I will take it out of your way at once. I
may want it. It should be with the others.
I know it as well as I know my snuff-box. It
was Aberthaw who put it in that corner; but

I had forgotten that it was lettered. The others are all numbered."

Of course Mr. Jellicorse was not weak enough to make the partner of his bosom the partner of his business; and much as she longed to know why he had put an unusual question to her, she trusted to the future for discovery of that point. She left him, and he with no undue haste—for the business, after all, was not his own—began to follow out his train of thought, in manner much as follows:—

" This is that old Duncombe's writing, ' Dunder-headed Duncombe,' as he used to be called in his lifetime, but ' Long-headed Duncombe' afterwards. None but his wife knew whether he was a wise man, or a wise-acre. Perhaps either, according to the treatment he received. Richard Yordas treated him badly; that may have made him wiser. V. b. c. means ' vide box C,' unless I am greatly mistaken. He wrote those letters as plainly and clearly as he could against this power of appointment as recited here. But afterwards, with knife and pounce, he scraped them out, as now becomes plain with this magnifying glass; probably he did so when all these archives, as he used to call them, were rudely ordered over to my predecessor. A nice bit of revenge, if my suspicions are correct; and a pretty confusion will follow it."

The lawyer's suspicions proved too correct. He took that box to his private room, and with some trouble unlocked it. A damp and musty smell came forth, as when a man delves a potato-bury; and then appeared layers of parchment yellow and brown, in and out with one another, according to the curing of the sheepskin, perhaps, or the age of the sheep when he began to die; skins much older than any man's who handled them, and dryer than the brains of any lawyer.

"Anno Jacobi tertio, and Quadragesimo Elisabethæ! How nice it sounds!" Mr. Jellicorse exclaimed; "they ought all to go in, and be charged for. People to be satisfied with sixty years' title! Why, bless the Lord, I am sixty-eight myself, and could buy and sell the grammar-school at eight years old. It is no security, no security at all. What did the learned Bacupiston say? 'If a rogue only lives to be a hundred and eleven, he may have been for ninety years dis-seised, and nobody alive to know it!'"

Older and older grew the documents as the lawyer's hand travelled downwards; any flaw or failure must have been healed by lapse of time long and long ago; dust and grime and mildew thickened, ink became paler, and contractions more contorted; it was rather an antiquary's business now than a lawyer's to decipher them.

"What a fool I am!" the solicitor thought. "My cuffs will never wash white again, and all I have found is a mare's nest. However, I'll go to the bottom now. There may be a gold seal, they used to put them in with the deeds three hundred years ago. A charter of Edward the Fourth, I declare! Ah, the Yordases were Yorkists—halloa, what is here? By the Touchstone of Shepherd I was right after all! Well done, long-headed Duncombe!"

From the very bottom of the box he took a parchment comparatively fresh and new, endorsed "Appointment by Richard Yordas, Esquire, and Eleanor his wife, of lands and heredits at Scargate and elsewhere in the county of York, dated Nov. 15th, A.D. 1751." Having glanced at the signatures and seals, Mr. Jellicorse spread the document, which was of moderate compass, and soon convinced himself that his work of the morning had been wholly thrown away. No title could be shown to Whitestone Farm, nor even to Scargate Hall itself, on the part of the present owners.

The appointment was by deed-poll, and strictly in accordance with the powers of the settlement. Duly executed and attested, clearly though clumsily expressed, and beyond all question genuine, it simply nullified (as concerned the better half of the property) the will which had cost Philip Yordas his life. For under this limitation Philip held a mere life interest, his father and mother giving all men to know by those presents that they did thereby from and after the decease of their said son Philip grant limit and appoint &c. all and singular the said lands &c. to the heirs of his body lawfully begotten &c. &c. in tail general, with remainder over, and final remainder to the right heirs of the said Richard Yordas for ever. From all which it followed that while Duncan Yordas, or child, or other descendant of his remained in the land of the living, or even without that if he having learned it had been enabled to bar

the entail and then sell or devise the lands
away, the ladies in possession could show no
title, except a possessory one, as yet unhal-
lowed by the lapse of time.

Mr. Jellicorse was a very pleasant-looking
man, also one who took a pleasant view of
other men and things; but he could not help
pulling a long and sad face, as he thought of
the puzzle before him. Duncan Yordas had
not been heard of among his own hills and
valleys since 1778, when he embarked for
India. None of the family ever had cared to
write or read long letters, their correspond-
ence (if any) was short, without being sweet
by any means. It might be a subject for
prayer and hope that Duncan should be gone
to a better world, without leaving hostages
to fortune here; but sad it is to say that
neither prayer nor hope produces any faith
in the Counsel who prepares "requisitions
upon title."

On the other hand, inquiry as to Duncan's
history since he left his native land would be
a delicate and expensive work, and perhaps
even dangerous, if he should hear of it, and
inquire about the inquirers. For the last
thing to be done from a legal point of view—

though the first of all from a just one—was to apprise the rightful owner of his unexpected position. Now Mr. Jellicorse was a just man; but his justice was due to his clients first.

After a long brown study he reaped his crop of meditation thus—"It is a ticklish job; and I will sleep three nights upon it."

CHAPTER IV.

DISQUIETUDE.

THE ladies of Scargate Hall were uneasy,
although the weather was so fine, upon this
day of early August, in the year now current.
It was a remarkable fact that in spite of the
distance they slept asunder, which could not
be less than five-and-thirty yards, both had
been visited by a dream, which appeared to
be quite the same dream, until examined
narrowly, and being examined grew more
surprising in its points of difference. They
were much above paying any heed to dreams,
though instructed by the patriarchs to do so;
and they seemed to be quite getting over the
effects, when the lesson and the punishment
astonished them.

Lately it had been established (although
many leading people went against it, and

threatened to prosecute the man for trespass) that here in these quiet and reputable places, where no spy could be needed, a man should come twice every week with letters, and in the name of the king be paid for them. Such things were required in towns perhaps, as corporations and gutters were; but to bring them where people could mind their own business, and charge them two groats for some fool who knew their names, was like putting a tax upon their christening. So it was the hope of many, as well as every one's belief, that the postman, being of Lancastrian race, would very soon be bogged, or famished, or get lost in a fog, or swept off by a flood, or go and break his own neck from a precipice.

The postman, however, was a wiry fellow, and as tough as any native, and he rode a pony even tougher than himself, whose cradle was a marsh, and whose mother a mountain, his first breath a fog, and his weaning-meat wire-grass, and his form a combination of sole-leather and corundum. He wore no shoes for fear of not making sparks at night, to show. the road, and although his bit had been a blacksmith's rasp, he would yield

to it only when it suited him. The postman,
whose name was George King (which con-
founded him with King George, in the money
to pay), carried a sword and blunderbuss, and
would use them sooner than argue.

Now this man and horse had come slowly
along, without meaning any mischief, to de-
liver a large sealed packet with sixteen pence
to pay put upon it, "to Mistress Philippa
Yordas, &c., her own hands, and speed, speed,
speed;" which they carried out duly by stop,
stop, stop, whensoever they were hungry, or
saw anything to look at. None the less for
that, though with certainty much later, they
arrived in good trim, by the middle of the
day, and ready for the comfort which they
both deserved.

As yet it was not considered safe to trust
any tidings of importance to the post, in such
a world as this was; and even were it safe,
it would be bad manners from a man of business. Therefore Mr. Jellicorse had sealed
up little, except his respectful consideration
and request to be allowed to wait upon his
honoured clients, concerning a matter of
great moment, upon the afternoon of Thursday then next ensuing. And the post had

gone so far, to give good distance for the money, that the Thursday of the future came to be that very day.

The present century opened with a chilly and dark year, following three bad seasons of severity and scarcity. And in the north-west of Yorkshire, though the summer was now so far advanced, there had been very. little sunshine. For the last day or two, the sun had laboured to sweep up the mist and cloud, and was beginning to prevail so far,·that the mists drew their skirts up and retired into haze, while the clouds fell away to the ring of the sky, and there lay down to abide their time. Wherefore it happened that "Yordas House" (as the ancient build-ing was in old time called) had a clearer view than usual of the valley, and the river that ran away, and the road that tried to run up to it. Now this was considered a won-derful road, and in fair truth it was wonder-ful, withstanding all efforts of even the Royal Mail pony to knock it to pieces. In its rapidity downhill it surpassed altogether the river, which galloped along by the side of it, and it stood out so boldly with stones of no shame, that even by moonlight nobody could

lose it, until it abruptly lost itself. But it
never did that, until the house it came from
was two miles away, and no other to be seen;
and so why should it go any further?

At the head of this road stood the old grey
house, facing towards the south of east, to
claim whatever might come up the valley,
sun, or storm, or columned fog. In the days
of the past it had claimed much more, goods,
and cattle, and tribute of the traffic going
northward; as the loopholed quadrangle for
impounded stock, and the deeply embrasured
tower showed. At the back of the house
rose a mountain spine, blocking out the
westering sun, but cut with one deep portal
where a pass ran into Westmoreland,—the
scaur-gate whence the house was named;
and through this gate of mountain often,
when the day was waning, a bar of slanting
sunset entered, like a plume of golden dust, and
hovered on a broad black patch of weather-
beaten fir-trees. The day was waning now,
and every steep ascent looked steeper, while
down the valley light and shade made longer
cast of shuttle, and the margin of the west
began to glow with a deep wine-colour, as
the sun came down — the tinge of many

mountains and the distant sea—until the sun himself settled quietly into it, and there grew richer and more ripe (as old bottled wine is fed by the crust) and bowed his rubicund farewell, through the postern of the scaurgate, to the old Hall, and the valley, and the face of Mr. Jellicorse.

That gentleman's countenance did not, however, reply with its usual brightness to the mellow salute of evening. Wearied and shaken by the long, rough ride, and depressed by the heavy solitude, he hated and almost feared the task which every step brought nearer. As the house rose higher and higher against the red sky and grew darker, and as the sullen roar of bloodhounds (terrors of the neighbourhood) roused the slow echoes of the crags, the lawyer was almost fain to turn his horse's head, and face the risks of wandering over the moor by night. But the hoisting of a flag, the well-known token—confirmed by large letters on a rock—that strangers might safely approach, inasmuch as the savage dogs were kennelled, this, and the thought of such an entry for his daybook, kept Mr. Jellicorse from ignominious flight. He was in for it now, and must carry it through.

In a deep embayed window of leaded glass,
Mistress Yordas and her widowed sister sat
for an hour, without many words, watching the
zigzag of shale and rock which formed their
chief communication with the peopled world.
They did not care to improve their access,
or increase their traffic; not through cold
morosity, or even proud indifference, but
because they had been so brought up, and so
confirmed by circumstance. For the Yordas
blood, however hot, and wild, and savage, in
the gentlemen, was generally calm, and good,
though stubborn, in the weaker vessels. For
the main part, however, a family takes its
character more from the sword than the
spindle; and their sword-hand had been as
that of Ishmael.

Little as they meddled with the doings of
the world, of one thing at least these stately
Madams — as the baffled squires of the
Riding called them—were by no means heed-
less. They dressed themselves according to
their rank, or perhaps above it. Many a
nobleman's wife in Yorkshire had not such
apparel; and even of those so richly gifted,
few could have come up to the purpose
better. Nobody, unless of their own sex,

thought of their dresses, when looking at them.

"He rides very badly," Philippa said; "the people from the lowlands always do. He may not have courage to go home to-night. But he ought to have thought of that before."

"Poor man! We must offer him a bed of course," Mrs. Carnaby answered; "but he should have come earlier in the day. What shall we do with him, when he has done his business?"

"It is not our place to amuse our lawyer. He might go and smoke in the Justice-room, and then Welldrum could play bagatelle with him."

"Philippa, you forget that the Jellicorses are of a good old county stock. His wife is a stupid, pretentious thing; but we need not treat him as we must treat her. And it may be as well to make much of him, perhaps, if there really is any trouble coming."

"You are thinking of Pet. By-the-bye, are you certain that Pet cannot get at Saracen? You know how he let him loose last Easter, when the flag was flying, and the poor man has been in his bed ever since."

"Jordas will see to that. He can be
trusted to mind the dogs well, ever since you
fined him in a fortnight's wages. That was
an excellent thought of yours."

Jordas might have been called the keeper,
or the hind, or the henchman, or the ranger,
or the porter, or the bailiff, or the reeve, or
some other of some fifty names of office, in
a place of more civilization, so many and so
various were his tasks. But here his professional name was the "dogman;" and he held
that office according to an ancient custom of
the Scargate race, whence also his surname
(if such it were) arose. For of old time and
in outlandish parts, a finer humanity prevailed, and a richer practical wisdom upon
certain questions. Irregular offsets of the
stock, instead of being cast upon the world
as waifs and strays, were allowed a place
in the kitchen-garden or stable-yard, and
flourished there without disgrace, while useful and obedient. Thus for generations here,
the legitimate son was Yordas, and took the
house and manors; the illegitimate became
Jordas, and took to the gate, and the minding
of the dogs, and any other office of fidelity.

The present Jordas was, however, of less

immediate kin to the owners, being only the son of a former Jordas, and in the enjoyment of a Christian name, which never was provided for a first-hand Jordas; and now as his mistress looked out on the terrace, his burly figure came duly forth, and his keen eyes ranged the walks and courts, in search of Master Lancelot, who gave him more trouble in a day sometimes, than all the dogs cost in a twelvemonth. With a fine sense of mischief this boy delighted to watch the road for visitors, and then (if barbarously denied his proper enjoyment and that of the dogs) he still had goodly devices of his own for producing little tragedies.

Mr. Jellicorse knew Jordas well, and felt some pity for him, because if his grandmother had been wiser, he might have been the master now; and the lawyer, having much good feeling, liked not to make a groom of him. Jordas, however, knew his place, and touched his hat respectfully, then helped the solicitor to dismount, the which was sorely needed.

"You came not by the way of the ford, sir?" the dogman asked, while considering the leathers; "the water is down; you might have saved three miles."

"Better lose thirty than my life. Will any of your men, Master Jordas, show me a room, where I may prepare to wait upon your ladies?"

Mr. Jellicorse walked through the old arched gate of the reever's court, and was shown to a room, where he unpacked his valise, and changed his riding-clothes, and refreshed himself. A jug of Scargate ale was brought to him, and a bottle of foreign wine, with the cork drawn, lest he should hesitate; also a cold pie, bread and butter, and a small case-bottle of some liqueur. He was not hungry, for his wife had cared to victual him well for the journey; but for fear of offence he ate a morsel, found it good, and ate some more. Then after a sip or two of the liqueur, and a glance or two at his black silk stockings, buckled shoes, and best small-clothes, he felt himself fit to go before a Duchess, as once upon a time he had actually done, and expressed himself very well indeed, according to the dialogue delivered, whenever he told the story about it every day.

Welldrum, the butler, was waiting for him, a man who had his own ideas, and was going to be put upon by nobody. "If my father

could only come to life for one minute, he
would spend it in kicking that man," Mrs.
Carnaby had exclaimed about him, after carefully shutting the door; but he never showed
airs before Miss Yordas.

"Come along, sir," Welldrum said, after
one professional glance at the tray, to ascer-
tain his residue. "My ladies have been
waiting this half-hour; and for sure, sir, you
looks wonderful! This way, sir, and have a
care of them oak faggots. My ladies, Lawyer
Jellicorse!"

CHAPTER V.

DECISION.

THE sun was well down and away behind the great fell at the back of the house, and the large and heavily furnished room was feebly lit by four wax candles, and the glow of the west reflected as a gleam into eastern windows. The lawyer was pleased to have it so, and to speak with a dimly lighted face. The ladies looked beautiful; that was all that Mr. Jellicorse could say, when cross-examined by his wife next day concerning their lace and velvet. Whether they wore lace or net, was almost more than he could say, for he did not heed such trifles; but velvet was within his knowledge (though not the colour or the shape), because he thought it hot for summer, until he remembered what the climate was. Really he could say nothing

more, except that they looked beautiful; and
when Mrs. Jellicorse jerked her head, he said
that he only meant, of course, considering
their time of life.

The ladies saw his admiration, and felt
that it was but natural. Mrs. Carnaby came
forward kindly, and offered him a nice warm
hand; while the elder sister was content to
bow, and thank him for coming, and hope
that he was well. As yet it had not become
proper for a gentleman, visiting ladies, to
yawn, and throw himself into the nearest
chair, and cross his legs, and dance one foot,
and ask how much the toy-terrier cost. Mr.
Jellicorse made a fine series of bows, not
without a scrape or two, which showed his
goodly calf; and after that he waited for the
gracious invitation to sit down.

" If I understood your letter clearly," Mistress Yordas began, when these little rites were
duly ˄ accomplished, " you have something
important to tell us concerning our poor
property here. A small property, Mr. Jellicorse, compared with that of the Duke of
Lunedale, but perhaps a little longer in one
family."

" The duke is a new-fangled interloper,"

replied hypocritical Jellicorse, though no other duke was the husband of the duchess of whom he indited daily; "properties of that sort come and go, and only tradesmen notice it. Your estates have been longer in the seisin of one family, madam, than any other in the Riding, or perhaps in Yorkshire."

"We never seized them!" cried Mrs. Carnaby, being sensitive as to ancestral thefts, through tales about cattle-lifting; "you must be aware that they came to us by grant from the Crown, or even before there was any Crown to grant them."

"I beg your pardon for using a technical word, without explaining it. Seisin is a legal word, which simply means possession, or rather the bodily holding of a thing, and is used especially of corporeal hereditaments. You ladies have seisin of this house and lands, although you never seized them."

"The last thing we would think of doing," answered Mrs. Carnaby, who was more impulsive than her sister, also less straight-forward. "How often we have wished that our poor lost brother had not been deprived of them! But our father's will was sacred, and you told us we were helpless. We struggled, as you know; but we could do nothing."

"That is the question which brought me here," the lawyer said very quietly, at the same time producing a small roll of parchment sealed in cartridge paper; "last week I discovered a document which I am forced to submit to your judgment. Shall I read it to you, or tell its purport briefly?"

"Whatever it may be, it cannot in any way alter our conclusions. Our conclusions have never varied, however deeply they may have grieved us. We were bound to do justice to our dear father."

"Certainly, madam; and you did it. Also, as I know, you did it as kindly as possible towards other relatives, and you only met with perversity. I had the honour of preparing your respected father's will, a model of clearness and precision, considering —considering the time afforded, and other disturbing influences. I know for a fact, that a copy was laid before the finest drafts-man in London, by—by those who were displeased with it, and his words were, 'Beautiful, beautiful! Every word of it holds water.' Now that, madam, cannot be said of many, indeed of not one in—"

"Pardon me for interrupting you, but I have always understood you to speak highly of it. And in such a case, what can be the matter?"

"The matter of all matters, madam, is that the testator should have disposing power."

"He could dispose of his own property as he was disposed, you mean."

"You misapprehend me," Mr. Jellicorse now was in his element, for he loved to lecture—an absurdity just coming into vogue—"Indulge me one moment. I take this silver dish, for instance; it is in my hands, I have the use of it; but can I give it to either of you ladies?"

"Not very well, because it belongs to us already."

"You misapprehend me. I cannot give it, because it is not mine to give." Mrs. Carnaby looked puzzled.

"Eliza, allow me," said Mistress Yordas, in her stiffer manner, and now for the first time interfering; "Mr. Jellicorse assures us that his language is a model of clearness and

precision ; perhaps he will prove it by telling
us now, in plain words, what his meaning
is."

"What I mean, madam, is that your
respected father could devise you a part only
of this property; because the rest was not
his to devise. He only had a life-interest in
it."

" His will therefore fails as to some part of
the property ? How much, and what part, if
you please ? "

" The larger and better part of the estates,
including this house and grounds, and the
home-farm."

Mrs. Carnaby started and began to speak ;
but her sister moved only to stop her, and
showed no signs of dismay or anger.

" For fear of putting too many questions
at once," she said, with a slight bow and a
smile, " let me beg you to explain, as shortly
as possible, this very surprising matter."

Mr. Jellicorse watched her with some suspicion, because she called it so surprising,
yet showed so little surprise herself. For a
moment he thought that she must have heard
of the document now in his hands ; but he
very soon saw that it could not be so. It

was only the ancient Yordas pride, perversity, and stiffneckedness. And even Mrs. Carnaby, strengthened by the strength of her sister, managed to look as if nothing more than a tale of some tenant were pending. But this, or ten times this, availed not to deceive Mr. Jellicorse. That gentleman, having seen much of the world, whispered to himself that this was all "high jinks," felt himself placed on the stool of authority, and even ventured upon a pinch of snuff. This was unwise, and cost him dear, for the ladies would not have been true to their birth, if they had not stored it against him.

He, however, with a friendly mind, and a tap now and then upon his document, to give emphasis to his story, recounted the whole of it, and set forth how much was come of it already, and how much it might lead to. To Scargate Hall, and the better part of the property always enjoyed therewith, Philippa Yordas, and Eliza Carnaby, had no claim whatever, except on the score of possession, until it could be shown that their brother Duncan was dead, without any heirs or assignment (which might have come to pass through a son adult), and even so, his widow might come forward and give trouble. Concerning all that. there was time enough to think; but something must be done at once to cancel the bargain with Sir Walter Carnaby, without letting his man of law get scent of the fatal defect in title. And now that the ladies knew all, what did they say ?

In answer to this, the ladies were inclined to put the whole blame upon him, for not having managed matters better; and when he had shown that the whole of it was done before he had anything to do with it, they were firmly convinced that he ought to have known it, and found a proper remedy. And in the finished manner of well-born ladies, they gave him to know, without a strong expression, that such an atrocity was a black stain on every legal son of Satan, living, dead, or still to issue from Gerizim.

"That cannot affect the title now, I assure you, madam, that it cannot," the unfortunate lawyer exclaimed at last, "and as for damages, poor old Duncombe has left no representatives, even if an action would lie now which is simply out of the question. On my part no neglect can be shown, and indeed for your knowledge of the present state of things, if humbly I may say so, you are wholly indebted to my zeal."

"Sir, I heartily wish," Mrs. Carnaby replied, "that your zeal had been exhausted on your own affairs."

"Eliza, Mr. Jellicorse has acted well, and we cannot feel too much obliged to him." Miss Yordas, having humour of a sort, smiled faintly at the double meaning of her own words, which was not intended. "Whatever is right must be done of course, according to the rule of our family. In such a case it appears to me that mere niceties of laws, and quips and quirks, are entirely subordinate to high sense of honour. The first consideration must be thoroughly unselfish and pure justice."

The lawyer looked at her with admiration. He was capable of large sentiments. And yet a faint shadow of disappointment lingered in the folios of his heart,—there might have been such a very grand long suit, upon which his grandson (to be born next month) might have been enabled to settle for life, and bring up a legal family. Justice, however, was justice, and more noble than even such prospects. So he bowed his head, and took another pinch of snuff.

But Mrs. Carnaby (who had wept a little, in a place beyond the candlelight) came back with a passionate flush in her eyes, and a resolute bearing of her well-formed neck.

"Philippa, I am amazed at you," she said. "Mr. Jellicorse, my share is equal with my sister's, and more, because my son comes after me. Whatever she may do, I will never yield a pin's point of my rights, and leave my son a beggar. Philippa, would you make Pet a beggar? And his turtle in bed, before the sun is on the window, and his sturgeon-jelly when he gets out of bed! There never was any one, by a good Providence, less sent into the world to be a beggar."

Mrs. Carnaby, having discharged her meaning, began to be overcome by it. She sat down, in fear of hysteria, but with her mind made up to stop it; while the gallant Jellicorse was swept away by her eloquence, mixed with professional views. But it came home to him, from experience with his wife, that the less he said the wiser. But while he moved about, and almost danced, in his strong desire to be useful, there was another who sat quite still, and meant to have the final say.

"From some confusion of ideas, I suppose, or possibly through my own fault," Philippa Yordas said, with less contempt in her voice than in her mind; "it seems that I cannot make my meaning clear, even to my own sister. I said that we first must do the right, and scorn all legal subtleties. That we must maintain unselfish justice, and high sense of honour. Can there be any doubt what these dictate? What sort of daughters should we be, if we basely betrayed our own father's will?"

"Excellent madam," the lawyer said, "that view of the case never struck me. But there is a great deal in it."

"Oh, Philippa, how noble you are!" her sister Eliza cried; and cried no more, so far as tears go, for a long time afterwards.

CHAPTER VI.

ANERLEY FARM.

On the eastern coast of the same great
county, at more than ninety miles of distance
for a homing pigeon, and some hundred and
twenty for a carriage from the Hall of Yordas,
there was in those days, and there still may be
found, a property of no vast size, snug, however, and of good repute, and called univer-
sally "Anerley Farm." How long it has
borne that name, it knows not, neither cares
to moot the question; and there lives no
antiquary of enough antiquity to decide it. A
place of smiling hope, and comfort, and content with quietude; no memory of man about
it runneth to the contrary; while every ox,
and horse, and sheep, and fowl, and frisky
porker is full of warm domestic feeling and
each homely virtue.

For this land, like a happy country, has
escaped, for years and years, the affliction of
much history. It has not felt the desolating
tramp of lawyer or land-agent, nor been bom-
barded by fine and recovery, lease and release,
bargain and sale, Doe and Roe and Geoffrey
Styles, and the rest of the pitiless shower of
slugs, ending with a charge of Demons.
Blows, and blights, and plagues of that sort
have not come to Anerley, nor any other
drain of nurture to exhaust the green of
meadow and the gold of harvest. Here
stands the homestead, and here lies the
meadow-land; there walk the kine (having
no call to run), and yonder the wheat in the
hollow of the hill, bowing to a silvery stroke
of the wind, is touched with a promise of
increasing gold.

As good as the cattle and the crops themselves are the people that live upon them;
or at least, in a fair degree, they try to be so;
though not of course so harmless, or faithful,
or peaceful, or charitable. But still, in pro-
portion, they may be called as good; and in
fact they believe themselves much better.
And this from no conceit of any sort, beyond
what is indispensable; for nature not only

enables but compels a man to look down upon
his betters.

From generation to generation, man, and
beast, and house, and land, have gone on in
succession here, replacing, following, renewing, repairing and being repaired, demanding
and getting more support, with such judicious
give-and-take, and thoroughly good understanding, that now in the August of this
year, when Scargate Hall is full of care, and
afraid to cart a load of dung, Anerley Farm is
quite at ease, and in the very best of heart,
man, and horse, and land, and crops, and the
cock that crows the time of day.   Nevertheless, no acre yet in Yorkshire, or in the whole
wide world, has ever been so farmed or fenced,
as to exclude the step of change.

From father to son the good lands had
passed, without even a will to disturb them,
except at distant intervals; and the present
owner was Stephen Anerley, a thrifty and
well-to-do Yorkshire farmer of the olden type.
Master Anerley was turned quite lately of his
fifty-second year, and hopeful (if so pleased
the Lord) to turn a good many more years
yet, as a strong horse works his furrow.
For he was strong and of a cheerful face,

ruddy, square, and steadfast, built up also
with firm body to a wholesome stature,
and able to show the best man on the farm
the way to swing a pitchfork. Yet might he
be seen, upon every Lord's day, as clean as a
new-shelled chestnut; neither at any time of
the week was he dirtier than need be. Happy
alike in the place of his birth, his lot in life,
and the wisdom of the powers appointed over
him, he looked up, with a substantial faith,
yet a solid reserve of judgment, to the Church,
the Justices of the Peace, spiritual lords and
temporal, and above all His Majesty George
the Third. Without any reserve of judgment,
which could not deal with such low subjects,
he looked down upon every dissenter, every
pork-dealer, and every Frenchman. What
he was brought up to, that he would abide
by; and the sin beyond repentance, to his
mind, was the sin of the turn-coat.

With all these hard-set lines of thought, or
of doctrine (the scabbard of thought, which
saves its edge, and keeps it out of mischief),
Stephen Anerley was not hard, or stern, or
narrow-hearted. Kind, and gentle, and good
to every one who knew "how to behave
himself," and dealing to every man full jus-

tice—meted by his own measure—he was
liable even to generous acts, after being
severe and having his own way.. But if
anybody ever got the better of him, by lies,
and not fair bettering, that man had wiser
not begin to laugh inside the Riding. Stephen
Anerley was slow but sure; not so very keen,
perhaps, but grained with kerns of maxim'd
thought, to meet his uses as they came, and
to make a rogue uneasy. To move him from
such thoughts was hard; but to move him
from a spoken word had never been found
possible.

The wife of this solid man was solid and
well fitted to him. In early days, by her
own account, she had possessed considerable
elegance, and was not devoid of it even now,
whenever she received a visitor capable of
understanding it. But for home use that gift
had been cut short, almost in the honeymoon,
by a total want of appreciation on the part of
her husband. And now, after five-and-twenty
years of studying and entering into him, she
had fairly earned his firm belief that she was
the wisest of women. For she always agreed
with him, when he wished it; and she knew
exactly when to contradict him, and that was

before he had said a thing at all, and while
he was rolling it slowly in his mind, with a
strong tendency against it. In outdoor matters she never meddled, without being
specially consulted by the master; but indoors
she governed with watchful eyes, a firm hand,
and a quiet tongue.

This good woman now was five-and-forty
years of age, vigorous, clean, and of a very
pleasant look, with that richness of colour
which settles on fair women, when the fugitive beauty of blushing is past. When the
work of the morning was done, and the clock
ticked in the kitchen only ten minutes from
twelve, and the dinner was fit for the dishing,
then Mistress Anerley remembered as a rule
the necessity of looking to her own appearance. She went upstairs, with a quarter of
an hour to spare, but not to squander, and
she came down so neat that the farmer was
obliged to be careful in helping the gravy.
For she always sat next to him, as she had
done before there came any children, and
it seemed ever since to be the best place for
her to manage their plates and their manners
as well.

Alas! that the kindest and wisest of women

have one (if not twenty) blind sides to them; and if any such weakness is pointed out, it is sure to have come from their father. Mistress Anerley's weakness was almost conspicuous to herself—she worshipped her eldest son, perhaps the least worshipful of the family.

Willie Anerley was a fine young fellow, two inches taller than his father, with delicate features, and curly black hair, and cheeks as bright as a maiden's. He had soft blue eyes, and a rich clear voice, with a melancholy way of saying things, as if he were above all this. And yet he looked not like a fool; neither was he one altogether, when he began to think of things. The worst of him was that he always wanted something new to go on with. He never could be idle; and yet he never worked to the end which crowns the task. In the early stage he would labour hard, be full of the greatness of his aim, and demand everybody's interest, exciting also mighty hopes of what was safe to come of it. And even after that, he sometimes carried on with patience; but he had no perseverance. Once or twice he had been on the very nick of accomplishing something, and had driven home his nail—but there he let it spring back without clenching. " Oh, any fool can do that ! " he cried ; and never stood to it, to do it again, or to see that it came not undone. In a word, he stuck to nothing, but swerved about, here, there, and everywhere.

His father, being of so different a cast, and knowing how often the wisest of men must do what any fool can do, was bitterly vexed at the flighty ways of Willie, and could no more than hope, with a general contempt, that when the boy grew older he might be a wiser fool. But Willie's dear mother maintained, with great consistency, that such a perfect wonder could never be expected to do anything not wonderful. To this the farmer used to listen with a grim, decorous smile ; then grumbled, as soon as he was out of hearing, and fell to and did the little jobs himself.

Sore jealousy of Willie, perhaps, and keen sense of injustice, as well as high spirit and love of adventure, had driven the younger son Jack from home, and launched him on a seafaring life. With a stick and a bundle he had departed from the ancestral fields and lanes, one summer morning about three years since,

when the cows were lowing for the milk-pail,
and a royal cutter was cruising off the Head.
For a twelvemonth nothing was heard of him,
until there came a letter beginning, "Dear
and respected parents," and ending, "Your
affectionate and dutiful son, Jack." The
body of the letter was of three lines only,
occupied entirely with kind inquiries as to the
welfare of everybody, especially his pup, and
his old pony, and dear sister Mary.

Mary Anerley, the only daughter and the
youngest child, well deserved that best remembrance of the distant sailor; though Jack
may have gone too far in declaring (as he did
till he came to his love-time) that the world
contained no other girl fit to hold a candle to
her. No doubt it would have been hard to
find a girl more true and loving, more modest
and industrious; but hundreds and hundreds
of better girls might be found perhaps even
in Yorkshire.

For this maiden had a strong will of her
own, which makes against absolute perfection;
also she was troubled with a strenuous hate
of injustice—which is sure, in this world, to
find cause for an outbreak—and too active a
desire to rush after what is right, instead of

being well content to wait for that chary visitor.
And so firm could she be, when her mind was
set, that she would not take parables, or long
experience, or even kindly laughter, as a power
to move her from the thing she meant. Her
mother, knowing better how the world goes
on, promiscuously, and at leisure, and how
the right point slides away, when stronger
forces come to bear, was very often vexed by
the crotchets of the girl, and called her wayward, headstrong, and sometimes nothing
milder than " a saucy miss."

This, however, was absurd, and Mary
scarcely deigned to cry about it, but went
to her father, as she always did when any
weight lay on her mind. Nothing was said
about any injustice, because that might lead
to more of it, as well as be (from a proper
point of view) most indecorous. Nevertheless it was felt between them, when her pretty
hair was shed upon his noble waistcoat, that
they two were in the right, and cared very
little who thought otherwise.

Now it was time to leave off this ; for Mary
(without heed almost of any but her mother)
had turned into a full-grown damsel, comely,
sweet, and graceful. She was tall enough

never to look short, and short enough never
to seem too tall, even when her best feelings
were outraged; and nobody, looking at her
face, could wish to do anything but please
her; so kind was the gaze of her deep blue
eyes, so pleasant the frankness of her gentle
forehead, so playful the readiness of rosy lips
for a pretty answer or a lovely smile. But
if any could be found so callous and morose
as not to be charmed or nicely cheered by
this, let him only take a longer look, not
rudely, but simply in a spirit of polite inquiry;
and then would he see, on the delicate rounding of each soft and dimpled cheek, a carmine
hard to match on pallet, morning sky, or
flower-bed.

Lovely people ought to be at home in lovely
places; and though this cannot be so always,
as a general rule it is. At Anerley Farm the
land was equal to the stock it had to bear,
whether of trees, or corn, or cattle, hogs, or
mushrooms, or mankind. The farm was not
so large or rambling as to tire the mind or
foot, yet wide enough and full of change—
rich pasture, hazel copse, green valleys, fal-
lows brown, and golden breast-lands pillowing
into nooks of fern, clumps of shade for horse

or heifer, and for rabbits sandy warren, furzy cleve for hare and partridge, not without a little mere for willows and for wild ducks. And the whole of the land, with a general slope of liveliness and rejoicing, spread itself well to the sun, with a strong inclination towards the morning, to catch the cheery import of his voyage across the sea.

The pleasure of this situation was the more desirable, because of all the parts above it being bleak and dreary. Round the shoulders of the upland, like the arch of a great arm-chair, ran a barren scraggy ridge, whereupon no tree could stand upright, no cow be certain of her own tail, and scarcely a crow breast the violent air by stooping ragged pinions. So furious was the rush of wind, when any power awoke the clouds; or sometimes when the air was jaded with continual conflict, a heavy settlement of brackish cloud lay upon a waste of chalky flint.

By dint of persevering work, there are many changes for the better now, more shelter and more root-hold; but still it is a battle-ground of winds, which rarely change their habits, for this is the chump of the spine of

the Wolds, which hulks up at last into Flamborough Head.

Flamborough Head, the furthest forefront
of a bare and jagged coast, stretches boldly
off to eastward, a strong and rugged barrier.
Away to the north the land falls back, with
coving bends, and some straight lines of precipice and shingle, to which the German Ocean
sweeps, seldom free from sullen swell, in the
very best of weather. But to the southward
of the Head, a different spirit seems to move
upon the face of everything. For here is
spread a peaceful bay, and plains of brighter
sea more gently furrowed by the wind, and
cliffs that have no cause to be so steep, and
bathing-places, and scarcely freckled sands,
where towns may lay their drain-pipes undis-
turbed. In short, to have rounded that headland from the north is as good as to turn the
corner of a garden wall in March, and pass
from a buffeted back, and bare shivers, to a
sunny front of hope all as busy as a bee, with
pears spurring forward into creamy buds of
promise, peach-trees already in a flush of
tassel'd pink, and the green lobe of apricot
crouching under pointed buttons of unopened
leaf.

Below this Point, the gallant skipper of the British collier, slouching with a heavy load of grime for London, or waddling back in ballast to his native north, alike is delighted to discover storms ahead, and to cast his tarry anchor into soft grey calm. For here shall he find the good shelter of friends like-minded with himself, and of hospitable turn, having no cause to hurry, any more than he has, all too wise to command their own ships; and here will they all jollify together, while the sky holds a cloud, or the locker a drop. Nothing here can shake their ships, except a violent east wind, against which they wet the other eye; lazy boats visit them with comfort and delight, while white waves are leaping in the offing; they cherish their well-earned rest, and eat the lotus—or rather the onion—and drink ambrosial grog; they lean upon the bulwarks, and contemplate their shadows—the noblest possible employment for mankind—and lo, if they care to lift their eyes, in the south shines the quay of Bridlington, inland the long ridge of Priory stands high, and westward in a nook, if they level well a clear glass (after holding on the slope so many steamy ones), they may espy

Anerley Farm, and sometimes Mary Anerley
herself.

For she, when the ripple of the tide is fresh,
and the glance of the summer morn glisten-
ing on the sands, also if a little rocky basin
happens to be fit for shrimping, and only
some sleepy ships at anchor in the distance
look at her, fearless she—because all sailors
are generally down at breakfast—tucks up
her skirt, and gaily runs upon the accustomed
playground, with her pony left to wait for
her. The pony is old, while she is young
(although she was born before him) and now
he belies his name, "Lord Keppel," by start-
ing at every soft glimmer of the sea. Therefore now he is left to roam at his leisure above
high-water mark, poking his nose into black
dry weed, probing the winnow-casts of yellow
drift for oats, and snorting disappointment
through a gritty dance of sand-hoppers.

Mary has brought him down the old "Dane's
Dyke" for society rather than service, and
to strengthen his nerves with the dew of the
salt, for the sake of her Jack who loved him.
He may do as he likes, as he always does.
If his conscience allows him to walk home,
no one will think the less of him. Having

very little conscience at his time of life (after
so much contact with mankind), he considers
convenience only.   To go home would suit
him very well, but his crib would be empty
till his young mistress came; moreover there
is a little dog that plagues him, when his door
is open; and in spite of old age, it is something to be free; and in spite of all experience,
to hope for something good.   Therefore Lord
Keppel is as faithful as the rocks; he lifts
his long heavy head and gazes wistfully at
the anchored ships, and Mary is sure that the
darling pines for his absent master.

But she with the multitudinous tingle of
youth runs away rejoicing.   The crisping
power and brilliance of the morning are upon
her, and the air of the bright sea lifts and
spreads her, like a pillowy skate's egg.   The
polish of the wet sand flickers, like veneer
of maple-wood, at every quick touch of her
dancing feet.   Her dancing feet are as light
as nature and high spirits made them, not
only quit of spindle heels, but even free from
shoes and socks left high and dry on the
shingle.   And lighter even than the dancing
feet the merry heart is dancing, laughing at
the shadows of its own delight; while the

radiance of blue eyes springs, like a fount of brighter heaven; and the sunny hair falls, flows, or floats, to provoke the wind for playmate.

Such a pretty sight was good to see for innocence and largeness. So the buoyancy of nature springs anew in those who have been weary, when they see her brisk power inspiring the young, who never stand still to think of her, but are up and away with her, where she will, at the breath of her subtle encouragement.

CHAPTER VII.

A DANE IN THE DYKE.

Now, whether spy-glass had been used by any watchful mariner, or whether only blind chance willed it, sure it is that one fine morning Mary met with somebody. And this was the more remarkable, when people came to think of it, because it was only the night before that her mother had almost said as much.

"Ye munna gaw doon te t' sea be yersell," Mistress Anerley said to her daughter; "happen ye mought be one too many."

Master Anerley's wife had been at "boarding school," as far south as Suffolk, and could speak the very best of Southern English (like her daughter Mary) upon polite occasion. But family cares and farm-house life had partly cured her of her education, and from

troubles of distant speech she had returned
to the ease of her native dialect.

"And if I go not to the sea by myself,"
asked Mary, with natural logic, "why, who
is there now to go with me?" She was
thinking of her sadly-missed comrade, Jack.

"Happen some day perhaps, one too many."

The maiden was almost too innocent to
blush; but her father took her part as usual.

"The little lass sall gaw doon," he said,
"wheniver sha likes." And so she went
down the next morning.

A thousand years ago the Dane's Dyke
must have been a very grand entrenchment,
and a thousand years ere that perhaps it was
still grander; for learned men say that it is a
British work, wrought out before the Danes
had even learned to build a ship. Whatever,
however, may be argued about that, the wise
and the witless do agree about one thing—
the stronghold inside it has been held by
Danes, while severed by the dyke from inland
parts; and these Danes made a good colony
of their own, and left to their descendants
distinct speech and manners, some traces of
which are existing even now. The Dyke, ex-
tending from the rough north sea to the calmer

waters of Bridlington Bay, is nothing more
than a deep dry trench, skilfully following the
hollows of the ground, and cutting off Flamborough Head and a solid cantle of high land
from the rest of Yorkshire. The corner, so in-
tercepted, used to be and is still called " Little
Denmark ;" and the indwellers feel a large
contempt for all their outer neighbours. And
this is sad, because Anerley Farm lies wholly
outside of the Dyke, which for a long crooked
distance serves as its eastern boundary.

Upon the morning of the selfsame day that
saw Mr. Jellicorse set forth upon his return
from Scargate Hall, armed with instructions
to defy the Devil, and to keep his discovery
quiet—upon a lovely August morning of the
first year of a new century, Mary Anerley,
blithe and gay, came riding down the grassy
hollow of this ancient Dane's Dyke. This
was her shortest way to the sea, and the tide
would suit (if she could only catch it) for a
take of shrimps, and perhaps even prawns,
in time for her father's breakfast. And not
to lose this, she arose right early, and rousing
Lord Keppel, set forth for the spot where
she kept her net covered with sea-weed. The
sun, though up and brisk already upon sea

and foreland, had not found time to rout the
shadows skulking in the dingles. But even
here, where sap of time had breached the
turfy ramparts, the hover of the dew-mist
passed away, and the steady light was un-
folded.

For the season was early August still, with
beautiful weather come at last ; and the green
world seemed to stand on tip-toe to make
the extraordinary acquaintance of the sun.
Humble plants which had long lain flat stood
up with a sense of casting something off ; and
the damp heavy trunks which had trickled for
a twelvemonth, or been only sponged with
moss, were hailing the fresher light with
keener lines and dove-coloured tints upon
their smoother boles. Then conquering the
barrier of the eastern land-crest, rose the glorious sun himself, strewing before him trees
and crags in long steep shadows down the
hill. Then the sloping rays, through furze
and brushland, kindling the sparkles of the
dew, descended to the brink of the Dyke, and
scorning to halt at petty obstacles, with a
hundred golden hurdles bridged it, wherever
any opening was.

Under this luminous span, or through it

where the crossing gullies ran, Mary Anerley
rode at leisure, allowing her pony to choose
his pace. That privilege he had long secured,
in right of age, and wisdom, and remarkable
force of character. Considering his time of
life, he looked well, and sleek, and almost
sprightly; and so, without any reservation,
did his gentle and graceful rider. The maiden
looked well in a place like that, as indeed in
almost any place; but now she especially set
off the colour of things, and was set off by
them. For instance, how could the silver of
the dew-cloud, and golden weft of sunrise,
playing through the dapples of a partly wooded
glen, do better (in the matter of variety) than
frame a pretty moving figure in a pink checked
frock, with a skirt of russet murrey, and a
bright brown hat? Not that the hat itself
was bright, even under the kiss of sunshine,
simply having seen already too much of the
sun; but rather that its early lustre seemed
to be revived by a sense of the happy position
it was in; the clustering hair and the bright
eyes beneath it answering the sunny dance of
life and light. Many a handsomer face, no
doubt, more perfect, grand, and lofty, received
—at least if it was out of bed—the greeting

of that morning sun; but scarcely any prettier one, or kinder, or more pleasant; so gentle without being weak, so good-tempered without looking void of all temper at all.

Suddenly the beauty of the time and place was broken by sharp angry sound. Bang, bang, came the roar of muskets fired from the shore at the mouth of the Dyke, and echoing up the winding glen. At the first report the girl, though startled, was not greatly frightened; for the sound was common enough in the week when those most gallant volunteers, entitled the "Yorkshire Invincibles," came down for their annual practice of skilled gunnery against the French. Their habit was to bring down a red cock, and tether him against a chalky cliff, and then vie with one another in shooting at him. The same cock had tested their skill for three summers, but failed hitherto to attest it, preferring to return in a · hamper to his hens, with a story of moving adventures.

Mary had watched those Invincibles sometimes from a respectful distance, and therefore felt sure (when she began to think) that she had not them to thank for this little scare. For they always slept soundly in the first watch of the morning; and even supposing they had jumped up with nightmare, where was the jubilant crow of the cock? For the cock, being almost as invincible as they were, never could deny himself the glory of a crow, when the bullet came into his neighbourhood. He replied to every volley with an elevated comb, and a flapping of his wings, and a clarion peal, which rang along the foreshore, ere the musket-roar died out. But before the girl had time to ponder what this was, or wherefore, round the corner came somebody, running very swiftly.

In a moment Mary saw that this man had been shot at, and was making for his life away; and to give him every chance she jerked her pony aside, and called and beckoned; and without a word he flew to her. Words were beyond him, till his breath should come back, and he seemed to have no time to wait for that. He had outstripped the wind, and his own wind, by his speed.

"Poor man!" cried Mary Anerley, "what a hurry you are in! But I suppose you cannot help it. Are they shooting at you?"

The runaway nodded, for he could not spare a breath, but was deeply inhaling for another start, and could not even bow without hindrance. But to show that he had manners, he took off his hat. Then he clapped it on his head and set off again.

" Come back ! " cried the maid; " I can show you a place. I can hide you from your enemies for ever."

The young fellow stopped. He was come to that pitch of exhaustion in which a man scarcely cares whether he is killed or dies. And his face showed not a sign of fear.

"Look! That little hole—up there—by the fern; up at once, and this cloth over you ! "

He snatched it, and was gone like the darting lizard, up a little puckering side-issue of the Dyke, at the very same instant that three broad figures and a long one appeared at the lip of the mouth. The quick-witted girl rode on to meet them, to give the poor fugitive time to get into his hole, and draw the brown skirt over him. The dazzle of the sun, pouring over the crest, made the hollow a twinkling obscurity; and the cloth was just in keeping with the dead stuff around. The three broad men, with heavy fusils cocked, came up from the sea-mouth of the dyke, steadily panting, and running steadily with a

long enduring stride.   Behind them a tall
bony man with a cutlass, was swinging it
high in the air, and limping, and swearing
with great velocity.

"Coast-riders," thought Mary, "and he a
free-trader! Four against one is cowardice."

"Halt!" cried the tall man, while the rest
were running past her; "halt! ground arms;
never scare young ladies." Then he flourished
his hat, with a grand bow to Mary. "Fair
young Mistress Anerley, I fear we spoil your
ride.   But his Majesty's duty must be done.
Hats off, fellows, at the name of your king!
Mary, my dear, the most daring villain, the
devil's own son, has just run up here—
scarcely two minutes—you must have seen
him. Wait a minute, tell no lies—excuse me,
I mean fibs. Your father is the right sort.
He hates those scoundrels.   In the name of
his Majesty, which way is he gone?"

"Was it, oh, was it a man, if you please?
Captain Carroway, don't say so."

"A man?   Is it likely that we shot at a
woman? You are trifling.   It will be the
worse for you.   Forgive me—but we are in
such a hurry.   Whoa, whoa, pony."

"You always used to be so polite, sir, that

you quite surprise me. And those guns look so dreadful! My father would be quite astonished to see me not even allowed to go down to the sea, but hurried back here, as if the French had landed!"

"How can I help it, if your pony runs away so?" For Mary all this time had been cleverly contriving to increase and exaggerate her pony's fear, and so brought the gunners for a long way up the Dyke, without giving them any time to spy at all about. She knew that this was wicked from a loyal point of view; not a bit the less she did it. "What a troublesome little horse it is!" she cried. "Oh, Captain Carroway, hold him just a moment. I will jump down, and then you can jump up, and ride after all his Majesty's enemies."

"The Lord forbid! He slews all out of gear, like a carronade with rotten lashings. If I boarded him, how could I get out of his way? No, no, my dear, brace him up sharp, and bear clear."

"But you wanted to know about some enemy, captain. An enemy as bad as my poor Lord Keppel?"

"Mary, my dear, the very biggest villain!

A hundred golden guineas on his head; and half for you. Think of your father, my dear, and Sunday gowns. And you must have a young man, by-and-by, you know; such a beautiful maid as you are. And you might get a leather purse, and give it to him. Mary, on your duty, now?"

"Captain, you drive me so; what can I say? I cannot bear the thought of betraying anybody."

"Of course not, Mary dear; nobody asks you. He must be half a mile off by this time. You could never hurt him now; and you can tell your father that you have done your duty to the king."

"Well, Captain Carroway, if you are quite sure that it is too late to catch him, I can tell you all about him. But remember your word about the fifty guineas."

"Every farthing, every farthing, Mary; whatever my wife may say to it. Quick, quick! Which way did he run, my dear?"

"He really did not seem to me to be running at all; he was too tired."

"To be sure, to be sure, a worn-out fox! We have been two hours after him; he could

not run; no more can we. But which way
did he go, I mean?"

"I will not say anything for certain, sir;
even for fifty guineas. But he may have
come up here—mind, I say not that he did
—and if so, he might have set off again
for Sewerby. Slowly, very slowly, because
of being tired. But perhaps after all he was
not the man you mean."

"Forward, double quick! We are sure to
have him!" shouted the lieutenant—for his
true rank was that—flourishing his cutlass
again, and setting off at a wonderful pace,
considering his limp. "Five guineas every
man Jack of you. Thank you, young mistress, most heartily thank you. Dead or
alive, five guineas!"

With gun and sword in readiness, they all
rushed off; but one of the party, named
John Cadman, shook his head and looked
back with great mistrust at Mary, having no
better judgment of women than this, that he
never could believe even his own wife. And
he knew that it was mainly by the grace of
womankind that so much contraband work
was going on. Nevertheless it was out of his
power to act upon his own low opinions now.

The maiden, blushing deeply with the sense of her deceit, was informed by her guilty conscience of that nasty man's suspicions, and therefore gave a smack with her fern whip to Lord Keppel, impelling him to join, like a loyal little horse, the pursuit of his Majesty's enemies. But no sooner did she see all the men dispersed and scouring the distance with trustful ardour, than she turned her pony's head towards the sea again, and rode back round the bend of the hollow. What would her mother say if she lost the murrey skirt, which had cost six shillings at Bridlington fair? And ten times that money might be lost much better than for her father to discover how she lost it. For Master Stephen Anerley was a straight-backed man, and took three weeks of training in the Land Defence Yeomanry, at periods not more than a year apart, so that many people called him "Captain" now; and the loss of his suppleness at knee and elbow had turned his mind largely to politics, making him stiffly patriotic, and especially hot against all free-traders putting bad bargains to his wife, at the cost of the king and his revenue. If the bargain were a good one, that was no concern of his.

Not that Mary, however, could believe, or would even have such a bad mind as to imagine that any one, after being helped by her, would be mean enough to run off with her property. And now she came to think of it, there was something high and noble, she might almost say something down-right honest, in the face of that poor persecuted man. And in spite of all his panting, how brave he must have been, what a runner, and how clever to escape from all those cowardly coast-riders shooting right and left at him! Such a man steal that paltry skirt that her mother made such a fuss about! She was much more likely to find it in her clothes-press filled with golden guineas.

Before she was as certain as she wished to be of this (by reason of shrewd nativity) and while she believed that the fugitive must have seized such a chance and made good his escape towards North Sea or Flamborough, a quick shadow glanced across the long shafts of the sun, and a bodily form sped after it. To the middle of the Dyke leaped a young man smiling, and forth from the gully which had saved his life. To look at him, nobody ever could have guessed how fast he had fled, and how close he had lain hid. For he stood there as clean, and spruce, and careless, as even a sailor can be wished to be. Limber yet stalwart, agile though substantial, and as quick as a dart while as strong as a pike, he seemed cut out by nature for a true blue-jacket; but condition had made him a smuggler, or, to put it more gently, a free-trader. Britannia, being then at war with all the world, and alone in the right (as usual), had need of such lads, and produced them accordingly, and sometimes one too many. But Mary did not understand these laws.

This made her look at him with great surprise, and almost doubt whether he could be the man, until she saw her skirt neatly folded in his hand, and then she said, " How do you do, sir ? "

The free-trader looked at her with equal surprise. He had been in such a hurry, and his breath so short, and the chance of a fatal bullet after him so sharp, that his mind had been astray from any sense of beauty, and of everything else except the safety of the body. But now he looked at Mary, and his breath again went from him.

" You can run again now, I am sure of it,"

said she; " and if you would like to do anything to please me, run as fast as possible."

" What have I to run away from now?"
he answered in a deep sweet voice; " I run
from enemies, but not from friends."

" That is very wise. But your enemies are
still almost within call of you. They will
come back worse than ever, when they find
you are not there."

" I am not afraid, fair lady, for I understand their ways. I have led them a good
many dances before this; though it would
have been my last, without your help. They
will go on, all the morning, in the wrong
direction, even while they know it. Carroway is the most stubborn of men. He never
turns back; and the further he goes, the
better his bad leg is. They will scatter
about, among the fields and hedges, and call
one another, like partridges. And when they
cannot take another step, they will come
back to Anerley for breakfast."

" I dare say they will; and we shall be
glad to see them. My father is a soldier,
and his duty is to nourish and comfort the
forces of the king."

" Then you are young Mistress Anerley?

I was sure of it before. There are no two
such. And you have saved my life. It is
something to owe it so fairly."

The young sailor wanted to kiss Mary's
hand; but not being used to any gallantry,
she held out her hand in the simplest manner,
to take back her riding skirt; and he, though
longing in his heart to keep it, for a token or
pretext for another meeting, found no excuse
for doing so. And yet he was not without
some resource.

For the maiden was giving him a farewell
smile, being quite content with the good
she had done, and the luck of recovering her
property; and that sense of right, which in
those days formed a part of every good young
woman, said to her plainly that she must be
off. And she felt how unkind it was to keep
him any longer, in a place where the muzzle
of a gun, with a man behind it, might appear
at any moment. But he, having plentiful
breath again, was at home with himself to
spend it.

"Fair young lady," he began, for he saw
that Mary liked to be called a lady, because
it was a novelty; "owing more than I ever
can pay you already, may I ask a little more?

Then it is, that on your way down to the
sea, you would just pick up (if you should
chance to see it) the fellow-ring to this, and
perhaps you will look at this to know it by.
The one that was shot away flew against a
stone just on the left of the mouth of the
Dyke, but I durst not stop to look for it, and
I must not go back that way now. It is
more to me than a hatful of gold, though
nobody else would give a crown for it."

"And they really shot away one of your
ear-rings! Careless, cruel, wasteful men!
What could they have been thinking of?"

"They were thinking of getting what is
called 'blood-money.' One hundred pounds
for Robin Lyth. Dead or alive—one hundred
pounds."

"It makes me shiver, with the sun upon
me. Of course, they must offer money for—
for people. For people who have killed other
people, and bad things—but to offer a hundred
pounds for a free-trader, and fire great guns
at him to get it—I never should have thought
it of Captain Carroway."

"Carroway only does his duty. I like him
none the worse for it. Carroway is a fool, of
course. His life has been in my hands fifty

times; but I will never take it. He must be killed sooner or later, becauses he rushes into everything. But never will it be my doing."

"Then are you the celebrated Robin Lyth —the new Robin Hood, as they call him? The man who can do almost anything?"

"Mistress Anerley, I am Robin Lyth; but as you have seen, I cannot do much. I cannot even search for my own ear-ring."

"I will search for it, till I find it. They have shot at you too much. Cowardly, cowardly people! Captain Lyth, where shall I put it, if I find it?"

"If you could hide it for a week, and then —then tell me where to find it in the afternoon towards four o'clock, in the lane towards Bempton Cliffs. We are off to-night upon important business. We have been too careless lately, from laughing at poor Carroway."

"You are very careless now. You quite frighten me almost. The coast-riders might come back at any moment. And what could you do then?"

"Run away gallantly, as I did before; with this little difference that I should be fresh, while they are as stiff as nut-cracks. They have missed the best chance they ever had at me; it will make their temper very bad. If they shot at me again, they could do no good. Crooked mood makes crooked mode."

"You forget that I should not see such things. You may like very much to be shot at; but — but you should think of other people."

"I shall think of you only—I mean of your great kindness, and your promise to keep my ring for me. Of course you will tell nobody. Carroway will have me like a tiger, if you do. Farewell, young lady, for one week farewell."

With a wave of his hat he was gone, before Mary had time to retract her promise; and she thought of her mother, as she rode on slowly, to look for the smuggler's trinket.

CHAPTER VIII.

CAPTAIN CARROWAY.

FAME, that light-of-love trusted by so many, and never a wife till a widow—fame, the fair daughter of fuss and caprice, may yet take the phantom of bold Robin Lyth by the right hand, and lead it to a pedestal almost as lofty as Robin Hood's, or she may let it vanish like a bat across Lethe—a thing not bad enough for eminence.

However, at the date, and in the part of the world now dealt with, this great free-trader enjoyed the warm though possibly brief embrace of fame, having no rival, and being highly respected by all who were unwarped by a sense of duty. And blest as he was with a lively nature, he proceeded happily upon his path in life, notwithstanding a certain ticklish sense of being shot at

undesirably. This had befallen him now so
often, without producing any tangible effect,
that a great many people and especially the
shooters (convinced of the accuracy of their
aim) went far to believe that he possessed
some charm against wholesome bullet and
gunpowder. And lately even a crooked six-
pence dipped in holy water (which was still
to be had in Yorkshire) confirmed and doubled
the faith of all good people, by being declared
upon oath to have passed clean through him,
as was proved by its being picked up quite
clean.

This strong belief was of great use to him;
for, like many other beliefs, it went a very
long way to prove itself. Steady left-hands
now grew shaky in the level of the carbine,
and firm fore-fingers trembled slightly upon
draught of trigger, and the chief result of a
large discharge was a wale upon the marks-
man's shoulder. Robin, though so clever
and well-practised in the world, was scarcely
old enough yet to have learned the advantage
of misapprehension; which, if well handled
by any man, helps him in the cunning of
paltry things, better than a truer estimate.
But without going into that, he was pleased

with the fancy of being invulnerable; which not only doubled his courage, but trebled the discipline of his followers, and secured him the respect of all tradesmen. However, the worst of all things is, that just when they are establishing themselves, and earning true faith by continuance—out of pure opposition the direct contrary arises, and begins to prove itself. And to Captain Lyth this had just happened in the shot which carried off his left ear-ring.

Not that his body, or any fleshly member, could be said directly to have parted with its charm; but that a warning and a diffidence arose from so near a visitation. All genuine sailors are blest with strong faith; as they must be, by nature's compensation. Their bodies continually going up and down upon perpetual fluxion, they never could live if their minds did the same, like the minds of stationary landsmen. Therefore, their minds are of staunch immobility, to restore the due share of firm element. And not only that, but these men have compressed (through generations of circumstance), from small complications, simplicity. Being out in all weathers, and rolling about so, how can they

stand upon trifles ? Solid stays, and stan-
chions, and strong bulwarks are their need,
and not a dance of gnats in gossamer ;
hating all fogs, they blow not up with their
own breath misty mysteries, and gazing
mainly at the sky and sea, believe purely in
God and the devil.   In a word, these sailors
have religion.

Some of their religion is not well pronounced, but declares itself in over-strong
expressions.   However, it is in them, and at
any moment waiting opportunity of action—
a shipwreck or a grape-shot; and the chap-
lain has good hopes of them, when the doctor
has given them over.

Now one of their principal canons of faith,
and the one best observed in practice, is (or
at any rate used to be) that a man is bound
to wear ear-rings. For these, as sure tradition
shows, and no pious mariner would dare to
doubt, act as a whetstone in all weathers to
the keen edge of the eyes. Semble—as the
lawyers say—that this idea was born of great
phonetic facts, in the days when a seaman
knew his duty, better than the way to spell
it; and when, if his outlook were sharpened
by a friendly wring from the captain of the

watch, he never dreamed of a police-
court.

But Robin Lyth had never cared to ask
why he wore ear-rings. His nature was not
meditative. Enough for him that all the
other men of Flamborough did so; and·
enough for them that their fathers had done
it. Whether his own father had done so,
was more than he could say, because he
knew of no such parent; and of that other
necessity, a mother, he was equally ignorant.
His first appearance at Flamborough, though
it made little stir at the moment in a place of
so many adventures, might still be considered
unusual, and in some little degree, remarkable. So that Mistress Anerley was not
wrong when she pressed upon Lieutenant
Carroway how unwise it might be to shoot
him, any more than Carroway himself was
wrong in turning in at Anerley gate for
breakfast.

This he had not done without good cause
of honest and loyal necessity. Free-trading
Robin had predicted well the course of his
pursuers. Rushing eagerly up the Dyke,
and over its brim with their muskets, that
gallant force of Revenue-men steadily scoured

the neighbourhood; and the further they
went the worse they fared. There was not a
horse standing down by a pool, with his stiff
legs shut up into biped form, nor a cow
staring blandly across an old rail, nor a sheep
with a pectoral cough behind a hedge, nor a
rabbit making rustle at the eyebrow of his
hole, nor even a moot, that might either be a
man, or hold a man inside it—whom or which
those active fellows did not circumvent and
poke into. In none of these, however, could
they find the smallest breach of the strictest
laws of the revenue; until at last, having
exhausted their bodies, by great zeal both of
themselves and of mind, they braced them
again to the duty of going, as promptly as
possible, to breakfast.

For a purpose of that kind few better
places perhaps could be found than this
Anerley Farm, though not at the best of itself
just now, because of the denials of the season.
It is a sad truth about the hey-day of the
year, such as August is in Yorkshire—where
they have no spring—that just when a man
would like his victuals to rise to the mark of
the period, to be simple yet varied, exhila-
rating yet substantial, the heat of the summer

day defrauds its increased length for feeding.
For instance, to cite a very trifling point—at
least in some opinions—August has banished
that bright content and most devout resig-
nation which ensue the removal of a petted
pig from this troublous world of grunt. The
fat pig rolls in wallowing rapture, defying his
friends to make pork of him yet, and hugs
with complacence unpickleable hams. The
partridge among the pillared wheat, tenderly
footing the way for his chicks, and teaching
little balls of down to hop, knows how
sacred are their lives to others as well as to
himself; and the less paternal cock-pheasant
scratches the ridge of green-shouldered
potatoes, without fear of keeping them company at table.

But though the bright glory of the griddle
remains in suspense for the hoary mornings,
and hooks that carried woodcocks once, and
hope to do so yet again, are primed with dust
instead of lard, and the frying-pan hangs on
the cellar nail with a holiday gloss of raw
mutton suet—yet is there still some comfort
left, yet dappled brawn, and bacon streaked,
yet golden-hearted eggs, and mushrooms
quilted with pink satin, spiced beef carded

with pellucid fat, buckstone cake, and brown bread scented with the ash of gorse bloom— of these and more that pave the way into the good-will of mankind, what lack have fine farm-houses ?

And then again for the liquid duct, the softer and more sensitive, the one that is never out of season, but perennially brisk— here we have advantage of the gentle time that mellows thirst. The long ride of the summer sun makes men who are in feeling with him, and like him go up and down, not forego the moral of his labour, which is work and rest. Work all day, and light the rounded land with fruit and nurture, and rest at evening, looking through bright fluid, as the sun goes down.

But times there are when sun and man, by stress of work, or clouds, or light, or it may be some Process of the Equinox, make draughts upon the untilted day, and solace themselves in the morning. For lack of dew the sun draws lengthy sucks of cloud quite early, and men who have laboured far and dry, and scattered the rime of the night with dust, find themselves ready about 8 a.m. for the golden encouragement of gentle ale.

The farm-house had an old porch of stone, with a bench of stone on either side, and pointed windows trying to look out under brows of ivy; and this porch led into the long low hall, where the breakfast was beginning. To say what was on the table would be only waste of time, because it has all been eaten so long ago; but the farmer was vexed because there were no shrimps. Not that he cared half the clip of a whisker for all the shrimps that ever bearded the sea, only that he liked to seem to love them, to keep Mary at work for him. The flower of his flock, and of all the flocks of the world of the universe to his mind, was his darling daughter Mary; the strength of his love was upon her, and he liked to eat anything of her cooking.

His body was too firm to fidget; but his mind was out of its usual comfort, because the pride of his heart, his Mary, seemed to be hiding something from him. And with the justice to be expected from far clearer minds than his, being vexed by one, he was ripe for the relief of snapping at fifty others. Mary, who could read him, as a sailor reads his compass, by the corner of one eye, awaited with good content the usual result—an outbreak of words upon the indolent Willie, whenever that young farmer should come down to breakfast, then a comforting glance from the mother at her William, followed by a plate kept hot for him, and then a fine shake of the master's shoulders, and a stamp of departure for business. But instead of that, what came to pass was this.

In the first place, a mighty bark of dogs arose; as needs must be, where a man does his duty towards the nobler animals; for sure it is that the dogs will not fail of their part. Then an inferior noise of men, crying, "Good dog, good dog!" and other fulsome flatteries, in the hope of avoiding any tooth-mark on their legs; and after that a shaking down and settlement of sounds, as if feet were brought into good order, and stopped. Then a tall man, with a body full of corners, and a face of grim temper, stood in the doorway.

"Well, well, captain, now!" cried Stephen Anerley, getting up after waiting to be spoken to, "the breath of us all is hard to get, with doing of our duty, sir. Come ye in, and sit doon to table, and his Majesty's forces along o' ye."

"Cadman, Ellis, and Dick, be damned!"
the lieutenant shouted out to them; "you
shall have all the victuals you want, by-and-
by. Cross legs, and get your winds up.
Captain of the coast-defence, I am under
your orders, in your own house." Carroway
was starving, as only a man with long and
active jaws can starve; and now the appearance of the farmer's mouth, half full of a
kindly relish, made the emptiness of his own
more bitter. But happen what might, he resolved, as usual, to enforce strict discipline,
to feed himself first, and his men in proper
order.

"Walk in gentlemen, all walk in," Master
Anerley shouted, as if all men were alike, and
coming to the door with a hospitable stride;
"glad to see all of ye, upon my soul I am.
Ye've hit upon the right time for coming too;
though there might a' been more upon the
table. Mary, run, that's a dear, and fetch
your grandfather's big Sabbath carver.
Them peaky little clams a'most puts out
all my shoulder-blades, and wunna bite
through a twine of gristle. Plates for all
the gentlemen, Winnie lass! Bill, go and
drah the black jarge full o' yell."

The farmer knew well enough that Willie was not down yet; but this was his manner of letting people see that he did not approve of such hours.

"My poor lad Willie," said the mistress of the house, returning with a curtsey the brave lieutenant's scrape, "I fear he hath the rheum again, overheating of himself after sungate."

"Ay, ay, I forgot. He hath to heat himself in bed again, with the sun upon his coverlid. Mary, lof, how many hours was ye up?"

"Your daughter, sir," answered the lieutenant, with a glance at the maiden over the opal gleam of froth, which she had headed up for him; "your daughter has been down the Dyke before the sun was, and doing of her duty by the king and by his revenue. Mistress Anerley, your good health! Master Anerley, the like to you, and your daughter, and all of your good household." Before they had finished their thanks for this honour, the quart-pot was set down empty. "A very pretty brew, sir, a pretty brew indeed! Fall back, men! Have heed of discipline. A chalked line is what they want, sir. Mistress

Anerley, your good health again! The air is now thirsty in the mornings. If those fellows could be given a bench against the wall —a bench against the wall is what they feel for with their legs. It comes so natural to their—yes, yes, their legs, and the crook of their heels, ma'am, from what they were brought up to sit upon. And if you have any beer brewed for washing days, ma'am, that is what they like, and the right thing for their bellies. Cadman, Ellis, and Dick Hackerbody, sit down, and be thankful."

"But surely, Captain Carroway, you would never be happy to sit down without them. Look at their small clothes, the dust and the dirt! And their mouths show what you might make of them."

"Yes, madam, yes; the very worst of them is that. They are always looking out, here, there and everywhere, for victuals everlasting. Let them wait their proper time, and then they do it properly."

"Their proper time is now, sir. Winnie, fill their horns up. Mary, wait you upon the officer. Captain Carroway, I will not have anybody starve in my house."

"Madam, you are the lawgiver in your

own house. Men of the coast-guard, fall to
upon your victuals."

The lieutenant frowned horribly at his
men, as much as to say, "Take no advantage,
but show your best manners;" and they
touched their forelocks with a pleasant grin,
and began to feed rapidly; and verily their
wives would have said that it was high time
for them. Feeding, as a duty, was the order
of the day, and discipline had no rank left.
Good things appeared and disappeared, with
the speedy doom of all excellence. Mary,
and Winnie the maid, flitted in and out, like
carrier-pigeons.

"Now when the situation comes to this,"
said the farmer at last, being heartily pleased
with the style of their feeding and laughing,
"his Majesty hath made an officer of me,
though void of his own writing. Mounted
Fencibles, Filey Briggers, called in the foreign
parts 'Brigadiers.' Not that I stand upon
sermonry about it, except in the matter of his
Majesty's health, as never is due without
ardent spirits. But my wife hath a right to
her own way; and never yet I knowed her go
away from it."

"Not so, by any means," the mistress said,

and said it so quietly that some believed her;
" I never was so much for that. Captain, you
are a married man. But reason is reason, in
the middle of us all, and what else should I
say to my husband? Mary lass, Mary lof,
wherever is your duty? The captain hath
the best pot empty ! "

With a bright blush Mary sprang up to do
her duty. In those days no girl was ashamed
to blush; and the bloodless cheek savoured
of small-pox.

" Hold up your head, my lof," her father
said aloud, with a smile of tidy pride, and a
pat upon her back; " no call to look at all
ashamed, my dear. To my mind, captain,
though I may be wrong, however, but to my
mind this little maid may stan' upright in the
presence of downright any one."

" There lies the very thing that never should
be said. Captain, you have seven children, or
it may be eight of them justly. And the
pride of life—Mary, you be off ! "

Mary was glad to run away, for she liked
not to be among so many men. But her
father would not have her triumphed over.

" Speak for yourself, good wife," he said.
" I know what you have got behind, as well as

rooks know plough-tail. Captain, you never
heard me say that the lass were any booty,
but the very same as God hath made her, and
thankful for straight legs and eyes. Howso-
ever, there might be worse-favoured maidens,
without running out of the Riding."

"You may ride all the way to the city of
London," the captain exclaimed, with a clench
of his fist, " or even to Portsmouth, where my
wife came from, and never find a maid fit to
hold a candle for Mary to curl her hair
by."

The farmer was so pleased that he whispered something; but Carroway put his hand
before his mouth, and said, " Never, no never
in the morning ! " But in spite of that,
Master Anerley felt in his pocket for a key,
and departed.

"Wicked, wicked, is the word I use,"
protested Mrs. Anerley, " for all this fribble
about rooks and looks, and holding of candles,
and curling of hair. When I was Mary's
age—oh, dear ! It may not be so for your
daughters, captain; but evil for mine was
the day that invented those proud swinging-
glasses."

" That you may pronounce, ma'am, and I

will say Amen. Why, my eldest daughter in
her tenth year now—"

"Come, Captain Carroway," broke in the
farmer, returning softly with a square old
bottle; "how goes the fighting with the
Crappos now? Put your legs up, and light
your pipe, and tell us all the news."

"Cadman, and Ellis, and Dick Hackerbody," the lieutenant of the coast-guard
shouted, "you have fed well. Be off, men;
no more neglect of duty! Place an outpost
at fork of the Sewerby road, and strictly
observe the enemy; while I hold a council of
war with my brother-officer, Captain Anerley.
Half-a-crown for you, if you catch the rogue,
half-a-crown each, and promotion of two-
pence. Attention, eyes right, make yourselves
scarce! Well, now the rogues are gone, let
us make ourselves at home. Anerley, your
question is a dry one. A dry one; but this
is uncommonly fine stuff! How the devil
has it slipped through our fingers? Never
mind that, inter amicos—sir, I was at school
at Shrewsbury—but as to the war, sir, the
service is going to the devil, for the want of
pure principle."

The farmer nodded; and his looks declared

that to some extent he felt it. He had got the worst side of some bargains that week; but his wife had another way of thinking.

"Why, Captain Carroway, whatever could be purer? When you were at sea, had you ever a man of the downright principles of Nelson?"

"Nelson has done very well in his way; but he is a man who has risen too fast, as other men rise too slowly. Nothing in him; no substance, madam; I knew him as a youngster, and I could have tossed him on a marling-spike. And instead of feeding well, sir, he quite wore himself away. To my firm knowledge, he would scarcely turn the scale upon a good Frenchman of half of the peas. Every man should work his own way up, unless his father did it for him. In my time we had fifty men as good, and made no fuss about them."

"And you not the last of them, captain, I dare say. Though I do love to hear of the Lord's Lord Nelson, as the people call him. If ever a man fought his own way up—"

"Madam, I know him, and respect him well. He would walk up to the devil, with a sword between his teeth, and a boarder's pistol in each hand. Madam, I leaped in that condition, a depth of six fathoms and a half into the starboard mizen-chains of the French line-of-battle ship 'Peace and Thunder.'"

"Oh, Captain Carroway, how dreadful! What had you to lay hold with?"

"At such times a man must not lay hold. My business was to lay about; and I did it to some purpose. This little slash across my eyes struck fire, and it does the same now by moonlight."

One of the last men in the world to brag was Lieutenant Carroway. Nothing but the great thirst of this morning, and strong necessity of quenching it, could ever have led him to speak about himself, and remember his own little exploits. But the farmer was pleased, and said, "Tell us some more, sir."

"Mistress Anerley," the captain answered, shutting up the scar which he was able to expand, by means of a muscle of excitement; "you know that a man should drop these subjects, when he has got a large family. I have been in the Army and the Navy, madam, and now I am in the Revenue; but my duty is first to my own house."

" Do take care, sir, I beg you to be careful. Those free-traders now are come to such a pitch, that any day or night they may shoot you."

" Not they, madam. No, they are not murderers. In a hand-to-hand conflict they might do it, as I might do the same to them. This very morning my men shot at the captain of all smugglers, Robin Lyth of Flamborough, with a hundred guineas upon his head. It was no wish of mine, but my breath was short to stop them, and a man with a family like mine can never despise a hundred guineas."

" Why, Sophy," said the farmer, thinking slowly with a frown, " that must have been the noise come in at window, when I were. getting up this morning. I said, ' Why there's some poacher-fellow popping at the conies,' and out I went straight to the warren to see. Three gunshots, or might a' been four. How many men was you shooting at ? "

" The force under my command was in pursuit of one notorious criminal; that well-known villain, Robin Lyth."

" Captain, your duty is to do your duty.

But without your own word for it, I never would believe that you brought four gun-muzzles down upon one man."

"The force under my command carried three guns only. It was not in their power to shoot off four."

"Captain, I never would have done it in your place. I call it no better than unmanly. Now go you not for to stir yourself amiss. To look thunder at me is what I laugh at. But many things are done in a hurry, Captain Carroway, and I take it that this was one of them."

"As to that, no! I will not have it. All was in thorough good order. I was never so much as a cable's length behind, though the devil, some years ago, split my heel up, like his own, sir."

"Captain, I see it, and I ask your pardon. Your men were out of reach of hollering. At our time of life the wind dies quick, from want of blowing oftener."

"Stuff!" cried the captain. "Who was the freshest that came to your hospitable door, sir? I will foot it with any man for six leagues, but not for half a mile, ma'am. I depart from nothing. I said, 'Fire!' and

fire they did, and they shall again. What do
Volunteers know of the service?"

"Stephen, you shall not say a single other
word;" Mistress Anerley stopped her husband thus; "these matters are out of your
line altogether; because you have never
taken anybody's blood. The captain here
is used to it, like all the sons of 'Belial,
brought up in the early portions of the Holy
Writ."

Lieutenant Carroway's acquaintance with
the Bible was not more extensive than that of
other officers, and comprised little more than
the story of Joseph, and that of David and
Goliath; so he bowed to his hostess for her
comparison, while his gaunt and bristly countenance gave way to a pleasant smile. For
this officer of the British Crown had a face
of strong features, and upon it, whatever he
thought was told as plainly as the time of
day is told by the clock in the kitchen. At
the same time, Master Anerley was thinking that he might have said more than a host
should say, concerning a matter which, after
all, was no particular concern of his; whereas
it was his special place to be kind to any
visitor. All this he considered with a sound,

grave mind, and then stretched forth his right hand to the officer.

Carroway, being a generous man, would not be outdone in apologies. So these two strengthened their mutual esteem, · without any·fighting—which generally is the quickest way of renewing respect — and Mistress Anerley, having been a little frightened, took credit to herself for the good words she had used. Then the farmer, who seldom drank cordials, although he liked to see other people do it, set forth to see a man who was come about a rick, and sundry other business. But Carroway, in spite of all his boasts, was stiff, though he bravely denied that he could be ; and when the good housewife insisted on his stopping, to listen to something that was much upon her mind, and of great importance to the revenue, he could not help owning that duty compelled him to smoke another pipe, and hearken.

CHAPTER IX.

ROBIN COCKSCROFT.

NOTHING ever was allowed to stop Mrs. Anerley from seeing to the bedrooms. She kept them airing for about three hours, at this time of the sun-stitch—as she called all the doings of the sun upon the sky—and then there was pushing, and probing, and tossing, and pulling, and thumping, and kneading of knuckles, till the rib of every feather was aching; and then (like dough before the fire) every well belaboured tick was left to yeast itself awhile. Winnie, the maid, was as strong as a post, and wore them all out in bed-making. Carroway heard the beginning of this noise, but none of it meddled at all with his comfort; he lay back nicely in a happy fit of chair, stretched his legs well upon a bench, and nodded, keeping slow time with the breath-

ings of his pipe, and drawing a vapoury
dream of ease. He had fared many stony
miles afoot that morning; and feet, legs, and
body were now less young than they used to
be once upon a time. Looking up sleepily,
the captain had idea of a pretty young face
hanging over him, and a soft voice saying,
"It was me who did it all," which was very
good grammar in those days; "will you
forgive me? But I could not help it, and
you must have been sorry to shoot him."

"Shoot everybody who attempts to land,"
the weary man ordered drowsily; "Mattie,
once more, you are not to dust my pistols."

"I could not be happy without telling you
the truth," the soft voice continued, "because I told you such a dreadful story. And
now—oh! here comes mother!"

"What has come over you this morning,
child? You do the most extraordinary
things, and now you cannot let the captain
rest. Go round and look for eggs this very
moment. You will want to be playing fine
music next. Now, captain, I am at your
service, if you please, unless you feel too
sleepy."

"Mistress Anerley, I never felt more wide-awake in all my life. We of the service must snatch a wink whenever we can, but with one eye open; and it is not often that we see such charming sights."

The farmer's wife having set the beds to "plump," had stolen a look at the glass, and put on her second best Sunday cap, in honour of a real officer; and she looked very nice indeed, especially when she received a compliment. But she had seen too much of life to be disturbed thereby.

"Ah, Captain Carroway, what ways you have of getting on with simple people, while you are laughing all the time at them. It comes of the foreign war experience, going on so long, that in the end we shall all be foreigners. But one place there is that you never can conquer, nor Boneypart himself, to my belief."

"Ah, you mean Flamborough—Flamborough, yes! It is a nest of cockatrices."

"Captain, it is nothing of the sort. It is the most honest place in all the world. A man may throw a guinea on the cross-roads in the night, and have it back from Dr. Upandown any time within seven years. You ought to know by this time what they are; hard as it is to get among them."

"I only know that they can shut their mouths; and the devil himself—I beg your pardon, madam—Old Nick himself never could unscrew them."

"You are right, sir. I know their manner well. They are open as the sky with one another, but close as the grave to all the world outside them, and most of all to people of authority like you."

"Mistress Anerley, you have just hit it. Not a word can I get out of them. The name of the king—God bless him!—seems to have no weight among them."

"And you cannot get at them, sir, by any dint of money, or even by living in the midst of them. The only way to do it is by kin of blood, or marriage. And that is how I come to know more about them than almost anybody else outside. My master can scarcely win a word of them even, kind as he is, and well-spoken; and neither might I, though my tongue was tenfold, if it were not for Joan Cockscroft. But being Joan's cousin, I am like one of themselves."

"Cockscroft! Cockscroft? I have heard that name. Do they keep the public-house there?"

The lieutenant was now on the scent of duty, and assumed his most knowing air, the sole effect of which was to put everybody upon guard against him. For this was a man of no subtlety, but straightforward, downright, and ready to believe; and his cleverest device was to seem to disbelieve.

"The Cockscrofts keep no public-house," Mrs. Anerley answered, with a little flush of pride; "why, she was half-niece to my own grandmother, and never was beer in the family. Not that it would have been wrong, if it was. Captain, you are thinking of Widow Precious, licensed to the Cod with the hook in his gills. I should have thought, sir, that you might have known a little more of your neighbours having fallen below the path of life by reason of bad bank-tokens. Banking came up in her parts like dog-madness, as it might have done here, if our farmers were the fools to handle their cash with gloves on. And Joan became robbed by the fault of her trustees, the very best bakers in Scarborough, though Robin never married her for it, thank God! Still it was very sad, and scarcely bears describing of, and pulled them in the crook of this world's swing to a lower pitch than if

they had robbed the folk that robb.d and
ruined them. And Robin so was driven to
the fish again, which he always had hankered
after. It must have been before you heard of
this coast, captain, and before the long war
was so hard on us, that everybody about these
parts was to double his bags by banking,
and no man was right to pocket his own
guineas, for fear of his own wife feeling them.
And bitterly such were paid out for their
cowardice and swindling of their own bosoms."

"I have heard of it often, and it served
them right. Master Anerley knew where
his money was safe, ma'am!"

"Neither Captain Robin Cockscroft nor
his wife was in any way to blame," answered
Mrs. Anerley. "I have framed my mind to
tell you about them; and I will do it truly,
if I am not interrupted. Two hammers
never yet drove a nail straight, and I make
a rule of silence, when my betters wish to
talk."

"Madam, you remind me of my own wife.
She asks me a question, and she will not let
me answer."

"That is the only way I know of getting
on. Mistress Carroway must understand

you, captain. I was at the point of telling
you how my cousin Joan was married, before
her money went, and when she was really
good-looking. I was quite a child, and ran
along the shore to see it. It must have been
in the high summer-time, with the weather
fit for bathing, and the sea as smooth as a
duck-pond. And Captain Robin, being well-
to-do, and established with everything except
a wife, and pleased with the pretty smile and
quiet ways of Joan—for he never had heard of
her money, mind—put his oar into the sea and
rowed from Flamborough all the way to
Filey Brigg, with thirty-five fishermen after
him; for the Flamborough people make a
point of seeing one another through their
troubles. And Robin was known for the
handsomest man, and the uttermost fisher
of the landing, with three boats of his own,
and good birth, and long sea-lines. And
there at once they found my cousin Joan,
with her trustees, come overland, four wag-
gons and a cart in all of them; and after
they were married, they burned sea-weed,
having no fear in those days of invasions.
And a merry day they made of it, and rowed
back by the moonshine. For every one liked

and respected Captain Cockscroft on account
of his skill with the deep-sea lines, and the
openness of his hands when full—a wonderful quiet and harmless man, as the manner
is of all great fishermen. They had bacon
for breakfast whenever they liked, and a
guinea to lend to anybody in distress.

"Then suddenly one morning, when his
hair was growing grey, and his eyes getting
weary of the night work, so that he said his
young Robin must grow big enough to learn
all the secrets of the fishes, while his father
took a spell in the blankets, suddenly there
came to them a shocking piece of news. All his
wife's bit of money, and his own as well, which
he had been putting by from year to year, was
lost in a new-fangled Bank, supposed as
faithful as the Bible. Joan was very nearly
crazed about it; but Captain Cockscroft
never heaved a sigh, though thay say it was
nearly seven hundred guineas. 'There are
fish enough still in the sea,' he said; 'and the
Lord has spared our children. I will build
a new boat, and not think of feather-beds.'

"Captain Carroway, he did so, and everybody knows what befell him. The new boat,
built with his own hands, was called the

"Mercy Robin," from his only son and daughter, little Mercy and poor Robin. The boat is there as bright as ever, scarlet within, and white outside; but the name is painted off, because the little dears are in their graves. Two nicer children were never seen, clever, and sprightly, and good to learn; they never even took a common bird's nest, I have heard, but loved all the little things the Lord has made, as if with a foreknowledge of going early home to Him. Their father came back very tired one morning, and went up the hill to his breakfast, and the children got into the boat and pushed off, in imitation of their daddy. It came on to blow, as it does down there, without a single whiff of warning, and when Robin awoke for his middle-day meal, the bodies of his little ones were lying on the table. And from that very day Captain Cockscroft, and his wife, began to grow old very quickly. The boat was recovered without much damage; and in it he sits by the hour on dry land, whenever there is no one on the cliffs to see him, with his hands upon his lap, and his eyes upon the place where his dear little children used to sit. Because he has always taken whatever fell upon him gently;

and of course that makes it ever so much
worse, when he dwells· upon the things that
come inside of him."

"Madam, you make me feel quite sorry
for him," the lieutenant exclaimed, as she
began to cry. "If even one of my little ones
was drowned, I declare to you, I cannot tell
what I should be like. And to lose them all at
once, and as his own wife perhaps would say,
because he was thinking of his breakfast!
And when he had been robbed, and the world
all gone against him!· Madam, it is a long
time, thank God, since I heard so sad a tale."

"Now you would not, captain, I am sure you
would not," said Mistress Anerley, getting
up á smile, yet freshening his perception of
a tear as well; "you would never have the
heart to destroy that poor old couple, by
striking the last prop from under them. By
the will of the Lord, they are broken down
enough. They are quietly hobbling to their
graves, and would you be the man to come
and knock them on their heads?"

"Mistress Anerley, have you ever heard
that I am a brute and inhuman? Madam,
I have no less than seven children, and I
hope to have fourteen."

"I hope with all my heart you may. And you will deserve them all, for promising so very kindly not to shoot poor Robin Lyth."

"Robin Lyth! I never spoke of him, madam. He is outlawed, condemned, with a fine reward upon him. We shot at him to-day, we shall shoot at him again; and before very long we must hit him. Ma'am, it is my duty to the king, the Constitution, the service I belong to, and the babes 1 have begotten."

"Blood-money poisons all innocent mouths, sir, and breaks out for generations. And for it you will have to take three lives, Robin's, the captain's, and my dear old cousin Joan's."

"Mistress Anerley, you deprive me of all satisfaction. It is just my luck, when my duty was so plain, and would pay so well for doing of."

"Listen now, captain. It is my opinion, and I am generally borne out by the end, that instead of a hundred pounds for killing Robin Lyth, you may get a thousand for preserving him alive. Do you know how he came upon this coast, and how he has won his extraordinary name?"

"I have certainly heard rumours; scarcely any two alike. But I took no heed of them. My duty was to catch him; and it mattered not a straw to me, who or what he was. But now I must really beg to know all about · him, and what makes you think such things of him. Why should that excellent old couple hang upon him? and what can make him worth such a quantity of money? Honestly, of course, I mean; honestly worth it, ma'am, without any cheating of his Majesty."

"Captain Carroway," his hostess said, not without a little blush, as she thought of the king, and his revenue; "cheating of his Majesty is a thing we leave for others. But if you wish to hear the story of that young man, so far as known, which is not so even in Flamborough, you must please to come on Sunday, sir; for Sunday is the only day that I can spare for clacking, as the common people say. I must be off now; I have fifty things to see to. And on Sunday my master has his best things on, and loves no better than to sit with his legs up, and a long clay pipe lying on him down below his waist (or to speak more correctly, where it used to be,

as he might indeed almost say the very same
of me) and then not to speak a word, but
hear other folk tell stories, that might not
have made such a dinner as himself. And as
for dinner, sir, if you will do the honour to
dine with them that are no more than in the
volunteers, a saddle of good mutton fit for
the Body-guards to ride upon, the men with
the skins around them all turned up, will be
ready just at one o'clock, if the parson lets
us out."

"My dear madam, I shall scarcely care to
look at any slice of victuals until one o'clock
on Sunday, by reason of looking forward."

After all, this was not such a gross exaggeration, Anerley Farm being famous for its
cheer; whereas the poor lieutenant, at the
best of times, had as much as he could do to
make both ends meet; and his wife, though
a wonderful manager, could give him no
better than coarse bread, and almost coarser
meat.

"And, sir, if your good lady would oblige
us also—"

"No, madam, no!" He cried with vigorous
decision, having found many festive occasions
spoiled by excess of loving vigilance; "we

thank you most truly; but I must say ' no.'
She would jump at the chance; but a husband
must consider. You may have heard it
mentioned that the Lord is now considering
about the production of an eighth little
Carroway."

" Captain, I have not, or I should not so
have spoken. But with all my heart I wish
you joy."

" I have pleasure, I assure you in the
prospect, Mistress Anerley. My friends
make wry faces-; but I blow them away.
' Tush,' I say, ' Tush, sir; at the rate we
now are fighting, and exhausting all British
material, there cannot be too many, sir, of
mettle such as mine!' What do you say to
that, madam?"

" Sir, I believe it is the Lord's own truth.
And true it is also that our country should do
more to support the brave hearts that fight
for it."

Mrs. Anerley sighed, for she thought of her
younger son, by his own perversity launched
into the thankless peril of fighting England's
battles. His death at any time might come
home, if any kind person should take the
trouble even to send news of it; or he might

lie at the bottom of the sea unknown, even
while they were talking.

But Carroway buttoned up his coat and
marched, after a pleasant and kind farewell.
In the course of hard service, he had seen
much grief, and suffered plenty of bitterness,
and he knew that it is not the part of a man
to multiply any of his troubles but children.
He went about his work, and he thought of
all his comforts, which need not have taken
very long to count, but he added to their
score by not counting them, and by the self-
same process diminished that of troubles.
And thus upon the whole he deserved his
Sunday dinner, and the tale of his hostess
after it, not a word of which Mary was allowed to hear, for some subtle reason of her
mother's. But the farmer heard it all, and
kept interrupting so, when his noddings and
the joggings of his pipe allowed, or perhaps
one should say compelled him, that merely
for the courtesy of saving common time; it is
better now to set it down without them. Moreover there are many things well worthy of
production, which she did not produce, for
reasons which are now no hindrance. And
the foremost of those reasons is that the lady

did not know the things; the second that she
could not tell them clearly as a man might;
and the third and best of all, that if she
could, she would not do so. In which she
certainly was quite right; for it would have
become her very badly, as the cousin of Joan
Cockscroft (half removed, and upon the
mother's side), and therefore kindly received
at Flamborough, and admitted into the inner
circle, and allowed to buy fish at wholesale
prices, if she had turned round upon all these
benefits, and described all the holes to be
found in the place, for the teaching of a
Revenue officer.

Still, it must be clearly understood that
the nature of the people is fishing. They
never were known to encourage free-trading,
but did their very utmost to protect themselves; and if they had produced the very
noblest free-trader, born before the time of
Mr. Cobden, neither the credit nor the blame
was theirs.

CHAPTER X.

ROBIN LYTH.

HALF a league to the north of bold Flamborough Head, the billows have carved for themselves a little cove among cliffs which are rugged, but not very high. This opening is something like the grain-shoot of a mill, or a screen for riddling gravel, so steep is the pitch of the ground, and so narrow the shingly ledge at the bottom. And truly in bad weather and at high tides, there is no shingle ledge at all, but the crest of the wave volleys up the incline, and the surf rushes on to the top of it. For the cove, though sheltered from other quarters, receives the full brunt of north-easterly gales, and offers no safe anchorage. But the hardy fishermen make the most of its scant convenience, and gratefully call it "North Landing;"

albeit both wind and tide must be in good
humour, or the only thing sure of any landing
is the sea. The long desolation of the sea
rolls in with a sound of melancholy, the grey
fog droops its fold of drizzle in the leaden-
tinted troughs, the pent cliffs overhang the
flapping of the sail, and a few yards of pebble
and of weed are all that a boat may come
home upon harmlessly. Yet here in the old
time landed men who carved the shape of
England; and here, even in these lesser days,
are landed uncommonly fine cod.

The difficulties of the feat are these—to
get ashore soundly, and then to make it
good; and after that to clench the exploit by
getting on land, which is yet a harder step.
Because the steep of the ground, like a stair-
case void of stairs, stands facing you, and the
cliff upon either side juts up close, to forbid
any flanking movement, and the scanty scarp
denies fair start for a rush at the power of
the hill-front. Yet here must the heavy
boats beach themselves, and wallow and yaw
in the shingly roar, while their cargo and
crew get out of them, their gunwales swinging from side to side, in the manner of a
porpoise rolling, and their stem and stern

going up and down, like a pair of lads at
see-saw.

But after these heavy boats have endured all
that, they have not found their rest yet, without a crowning effort. Up that gravelly and
gliddery ascent, which changes every groove
and run at every sudden shower, but never
grows any the softer, up that the heavy boats
must make clamber somehow, or not a single
timber of their precious frames is safe. A
big rope from the capstan at the summit is
made fast, as soon as the tails of the jack-
asses (laden with three cwt. of fish apiece)
have wagged their last flick at the brow of
the steep; and then with "yo-heave-ho"
above and below, through the cliffs echoing
over the dull sea, the groaning and grinding
of the stubborn tug begin. Each boat has
her own special course to travel up, and her
own special berth of safety, and she knows
every jag that will gore her on the road, and
every flint from which she will strike fire.
By dint of sheer sturdiness of arms, legs, and
lungs, keeping true time with the pant and
the shout, steadily goes it with hoist and
haul, and cheerily undulates the melody of call,
that rallies them all with a strong will

together.   Until the steep bluff and the
burden of the bulk by masculine labour are
conquered, and a long row of powerful
pinnaces displayed, as a mounted battery,
against the fishful sea.   With a view to this
clambering ruggedness of life, all of these
boats receive from their cradle a certain
limber rake and accommodating curve, instead
of a straight pertinacity of keel, that so they
may ride over all the scandals of this arduous
world.   And happen what may to them,
when they are at home, and gallantly balanced
on the brow-line of the steep, they make a
bright show upon the dreariness of coastland,
hanging as they do above the gullet of the
deep.   Painted outside with the brightest of
scarlet, and inside with the purest white, at
a little way off, they resemble gay butterflies,
preening their wings for a flight into the depth.

Here it must have been, and in the middle
of all these, that the very famous Robin Lyth
—prophetically treating him, but free as yet
of fame, or name, and simply unable to tell
himself,—shone in the doubt of the early
day-light (as a tidy-sized cod, if forgotten,
might have shone) upon the morning of
St. Swithin, A.D. 1782.

The day and the date were remembered
long by all the good people of Flamborough,
from the coming of the turn of a long bad
luck and a bitter time of starving. For the
weather of the summer had been worse than
usual—which is no little thing to say—and
the fish had expressed their opinion of it by
the eloquent silence of absence. Therefore
as the whole place lives on fish, whether in
the fishy or the fiscal form, goodly apparel
was becoming very rare, even upon high
Sundays; and stomachs, that might have
looked well beneath it, sank into unobtrusive
grief. But it is a long lane that has no
turning; and turns are the essence of one
very vital part.

Suddenly over the village had flown the
news of a noble arrival of fish. From the
cross-roads and the public-house, and the
licensed head-quarters of pepper and snuff,
and the loop-hole where a sheep had been
known to hang, in times of better trade, but
never could dream of hanging now; also
from the window of the man who had had a
hundred heads (superior to his own) shaken
at him, because he set up for making breeches,
in opposition to the women, and showed a

few patterns of what he could do, if any man
of legs would trade with him,—from all these
head-centres of intelligence, and others not
so prominent but equally potent, into the
very smallest hole it went (like the thrill in a
troublesome tooth) that here was a chance
come of feeding, a chance at last of feeding.
For the man on the cliff, the despairing watch-
man, weary of fastening his eyes upon the sea,
through constant fog and drizzle, at length had
discovered the well-known flicker, the glassy
flaw, and the hovering of gulls, and had run
along Weighing Lane so fast, to tell his good
news in the village, that down he fell and
broke his leg, exactly opposite the tailor's
shop.   And this was on St. Swithin's eve.

There was nothing to be done that night
of course, for mackerel must be delicately
worked; but long before the sun arose, all
Flamborough, able to put leg in front of leg,
and some who could not yet do that, gathered
together where the landhold was, above the
incline for the launching of the boats. Here
was a medley, not of fisher-folk alone, and all
their bodily belongings, but also of the
thousand things that have no soul, and get
kicked about and sworn at much, because

they cannot answer. Rollers, buoys, nets, kegs, swabs, fenders, blocks, buckets, kedges, corks, buckie-pots, oars, poppies, tillers, sprits, gaffs, and every kind of gear (more than Theocritus himself could tell) lay about, and rolled about, and upset their own masters, here and there and everywhere, upon this half-acre of slip and stumble, at the top of the boat-channel down to the sea, and in the faint rivalry of three vague lights, all making darkness visible.

For very ancient lanterns, with a gentle horny glimmer, and loop-holes of large exaggeration at the top, were casting upon anything quite within their reach a general idea of the crinkled tin that framed them, and a shuffle of inconstant shadows, but refused to shed any light on friend or stranger, or clear up suspicions more than three yards off. In rivalry with these appeared the pale disc of the moon, just setting over the western highlands, and "drawing straws" through summer haze; while away in the north-east over the sea, a slender irregular wisp of grey, so weak that it seemed as if it were being blown away, betokened the intention of the sun to restore clear ideas of number and of

figure by-and-by. But little did anybody heed
such things; every one ran against everybody
else, and all was eagerness, haste, and bustle
for the first great launch of the Flamborough
boats, all of which must be taken in order.

But when they laid hold of the boat No. 7,
which used to be the " Mercy Robin," and
were jerking the timber shores out, one of
the men stooping under her stern beheld
something white and gleaming. He put his
hand down to it; and lo, it was a child, in
imminent peril of a deadly crush, as the boat
came heeling over. " Hold hard! " cried the
man, not in time with his voice, but in time
with his sturdy shoulder, to delay the descent
of the counter. Then he stooped underneath,
while they steadied the boat, and drew forth
a child in a white linen dress, heartily asleep
and happy.

There was no time to think of any children
now, even of a man's own fine breed, and the
boat was beginning much to chafe upon the
rope, and thirty or forty fine fellows were all
waiting, loth to hurry Captain Robin (because
of the many things he had dearly lost), yet
straining upon their own hearts, to stand
still. And the captain could not find his

wife, who had slipped aside of the noisy scene,
to have her own little cry, because of the
dance her children would have made, if they
had lived to see it.

There were plenty of other women running
all about to help, and to talk, and to give the
best advice to their husbands and to one
another; but most of them naturally had
their own babies, and if words came to action,
quite enough to do to nurse them. On this
account, Cockscroft could do no better, bound
as he was to rush forth upon the sea, than
lay the child gently aside of the stir, and
cover him with an old sail, and leave word
with an ancient woman for his wife when
found. The little boy slept on calmly still,
in spite of all the din and uproar, the song
and the shout, the tramp of heavy feet, the
creaking of capstans, and the thump of
bulky oars, and the crash of ponderous
rollers. Away went these upon their errand
to the sea, and then came back the grating
roar and plashy jerks of launching, the
plunging, and the gurgling, and the quiet
murmur of cleft waves.

That child slept on, in the warm good luck
of having no boat-keel launched upon him,

nor even a human heel of bulk as likely to prove fatal. And the ancient woman fell asleep beside him ; because at her time of life it was unjust that she should be astir so early. And it happened that Mistress Cockscroft followed her troubled husband down the steep, having something in her pocket for him, which she failed to fetch to hand. So every body went about its own business (according to the laws of nature), and the old woman slept by the side of the child, without giving him a corner of her scarlet shawl.

But when the day was broad and brave, and the spirit of the air was vigorous, and every cliff had a colour of its own, and a character to come out with ; and beautiful boats, upon a shining sea, flashed their oars, and went up waves, which clearly were the stairs of heaven ; and never a woman, come to watch her husband, could be sure how far he had carried his obedience in the matter of keeping his hat and coat on ; neither could anybody say what next those very clever fishermen might be after—nobody having a spy-glass—but only this being understood all round, that hunger and salt were the victuals for the day, and the children must chew the mouse-trap baits, until their dads came home again; yet in spite of all this, with lightsome hearts (so hope outstrips the sun, and soars with him behind her) and a strong will, up the hill they went, to do without much breakfast, but prepare for a glorious supper. For mackerel are good fish that do not strive to live for ever, but seem glad to support the human race.

Flamburians speak a rich burr of their own, broadly and handsomely distinct from that of outer Yorkshire. The same sagacious contempt for all hot haste and hurry (which people of impatient fibre are too apt to call "a drawl") may here be found, as in other Yorkshire, guiding and retarding well that headlong instrument the tongue. Yet even here there is advantage on the side of Flamborough—a longer resonance, a larger breadth, a deeper power of melancholy, and a stronger turn up of the tail of discourse, by some called the end of a sentence. Over and above all these, there dwell in "Little Denmark" many words, foreign to the real Yorkshireman. But alas! these merits of their speech cannot be embodied in print, without sad trouble, and result (if successful) still more saddening. Therefore it is proposed to let them speak in our inferior tongue, and to try to make them be not so very long about it. For when they are left to themselves entirely, they have so much solid matter to express, and they ripen it in their minds and throats with a process so deliberate, that strangers might condemn them briefly, and be off without hearing half of it. Whenever this happens to a Flamborough man, he finishes what he proposed to say, and then says it all over again to the wind.

When the "lavings" of the village, (as the weaker part, unfit for sea and left behind, were politely called, being very old men, women, and small children) full of conversation came, upon their way back from the tide, to the gravel brow now bare of boats, they could not help discovering there the poor old woman that fell asleep, because she ought to have been in bed, and by her side a little boy, who seemed to have no bed at all. The child lay above her in a tump of stubbly grass, where Robin Cockscroft had laid him; he had tossed the old sail off, perhaps in a dream, and he threatened to roll down upon the Granny. The contrast between his young, beautiful face white raiment, and readiness to roll, and the ancient woman's weary age (which it would be ungracious to describe), and scarlet shawl which she could not spare, and satisfaction to lie still—as the best thing left her now to do—this difference between them was enough to take anybody's notice, in the well-established sun.

"Nanny Pegler, get oop wi' ye!" cried a woman even older, but of tougher constitution. "Shame on ye to lig aboot so. Be ye browt to bed this toime o' loife?"

"A wonderful foine babby for sich an owd moother!" another proceeded with the elegant joke; "and foine swaddles too, wi' solid gowd upon 'em!"

"Stan' ivery one o' ye oot o' the way," cried ancient Nanny, now as wide awake as ever; "Master Robin Cockscroft gie ma t' bairn, an' nawbody sall hev him but Joan Cockscroft."

Joan Cockscroft, with a heavy heart, was lingering far behind the rest, thinking of the many merry launches, when her smart young Robin would have been in the boat with his father, and her pretty little Mercy, clinging to her hand, upon the homeward road, and

prattling of the fish to be caught that day ;
and inasmuch as Joan had not been able to
get face to face with her husband on the
beach, she had not yet heard of the stranger
child.   But soon the women sent a little boy to
fetch her, and she came among them, wondering what it could be.   For now a debate of
some vigour was arising upon a momentous
and exciting point, though not so keen by a
hundredth part, as it would have been twenty
years afterwards.   For the eldest old woman
had pronounced her decision.

"Tell ye wat, ah dean't think bud wat
yon bairn mud be a Frogman."

This caused some panic and a general
retreat ; for though the immortal Napoleon
had scarcely finished changing his teeth as
yet, a chronic uneasiness about Crappos
haunted that coast already, and they might
have sent this little boy to pave the way,
being capable of almost everything.

"Frogman ! " cried the old woman next to
her by birth, and believed to have higher
parts, though not yet ripe.   " Na, na, what
Frogman here?   Frogmen ha' skinny shanks,
and larks' heels, and holes down their bodies
like lamperns.   No sign of no frog aboot yon

bairn. As fair as a wench, and as clean as a
tyke. A' mought a'most been born in Flaambro'. And what gowd ha' Crappos got,
poor divils ? "

This opened the gate for a clamour of discourse ; for there surely could be no denial of
her words. And yet while her elder was
alive and out of bed, the habit of the village,
was to listen to her say, unless any man of
equal age arose to countervail it. But while
they were thus divided, Mrs. Cockscroft
came, and they stood aside. For she had
been kind to everybody, when her better
chances were ; and now in her trouble all
were grieved because she took it so to heart.
Joan Cockscroft did not say a word, but
glanced at the child with some contempt. In
spite of white linen and yellow gold, what
was he to her own dead Robin ?

But suddenly this child, whatever he was,
and vastly soever inferior, opened his eyes
and sent home their first glance to the very
heart of Joan Cockscroft. It was the exact
look—or so she always said—of her dead
angel, when she denied him something, for
the sake of his poor dear stomach. With an
outburst of tears, she flew straight to the

little one, snatched him in her arms, and tried to cover him with kisses.

The child, however, in a lordly manner, did not seem to like it. He drew away his red lips, and gathered up his nose, and passion flew out of his beautiful eyes, higher passion than that of any Cockscroft. And he tried to say something, which no one could make out. And women of high consideration, looking on, were wicked enough to be pleased at this, and say, that he must be a young lord, and they had quite foreseen it. But Joan knew what children are, and soothed him down so, with delicate hands, and a gentle look, and a subtle way of warming his cold places, that he very soon began to cuddle into her, and smile. Then she turned round to the other people, with both of his arms flung round her neck, and, his cheek laid on her shoulder, and she only said, "The Lord hath sent him."

CHAPTER XI.

DR. UPANDOWN.

THE practice of Flamborough was to listen
fairly to anything that might be said by any
one truly of the native breed, and to receive
it well into the crust of the mind, and let it
sink down slowly. But even after that, it
might not take root, unless it were fixed in
its settlement by their two great powers—the
law, and the Lord.

They had many visitations from the Lord,
as needs must be in such a very stormy place;
whereas of the law they heard much less;
but still they were even more afraid of that;
for they never knew how much it might cost.

Balancing matters (as they did their fish,
when the price was worth it, in Weighing
Lane), they came to the set conclusion, that the
law and the Lord might not agree, concerning

the child cast among them by the latter. A child or two had been thrown ashore before, and trouble once or twice had come of it ; and this child being cast, no one could say how, to such a height above all other children, he was likely enough to bring a spell upon their boats, if anything crooked to God's will were done; and even to draw them to their last stocking, if anything offended the providence of law.

In any other place, it would have been a point of combat, what to say and what to do, in such a case as this. But Flamborough was of all the wide world happiest in possessing an authority to reconcile all doubts. The law and the Lord—two powers supposed to be at variance always, and to share the week between them in proportions fixed by lawyers —the holy and unholy elements of man's brief existence, were combined in Flamborough parish in the person of its magisterial Rector. He was also believed to excel in the arts of divination and medicine too, for he was a full Doctor of Divinity. Before this gentleman must be laid, both for purse and conscience' sake, the case of the child just come out of the fogs.

And true it was that all these powers were centred in one famous man, known among the laity as "Parson Upandown." For the Reverend Turner Upround, to give him his proper name, was a Doctor of Divinity, a Justice of the Peace, and the present rector of Flamborough. Of all his offices and powers, there was not one that he overstrained; and all that knew him, unless they were thorough-going rogues and vagabonds, loved him. Not that he was such a soft-spoken man as many were, who thought more evil; but because of his deeds and nature, which were of the kindest. He did his utmost, on demand of duty, to sacrifice this nature to his stern position, as pastor and master of an up-hill parish, with many wrong things to be kept under. But while he succeeded in the form now and then, he failed continually in the substance.

This gentleman was not by any means a fool, unless a kind heart proves folly. At Cambridge, he had done very well, in the early days of the tripos, and was chosen fellow and tutor of Gonville and Caius College. But tiring of that dull round in his prime, he married, and took to a living; and the living

was one of the many upon which a perpetual
faster can barely live, unless he can go naked
also, and keep naked children. Now the
parsons had not yet discovered the glorious
merits of hard fasting, but freely enjoyed,
and with gratitude to God, the powers with
which He had blessed them. Happily Dr.
Upround had a solid income of his own, and
(like a sound mathematician) he took a wife
of terms coincident. So, without being
wealthy, they lived very well, and helped
their poorer neighbours.

Such a man generally thrives in the thriv-
ing of his flock, and does not harry them.
He gives them spiritual food enough to support them without daintiness, and he keeps
the proper distinction between the Sunday
and the poorer days. He clangs no bell of
reproach upon a Monday, when the squire
is leading the lady in to dinner, and the
labourer sniffing at his supper-pot, and he lets
the world play on a Saturday, while he works
his own head to find good words for the
morrow. Because he is a wise man who,
knows what other men are, and how seldom
they desire to be told the same thing, more
than a hundred and four times in a year.

Neither did his clerical skill stop here; for
Parson Upround thought twice about it, before he said anything to rub sore consciences,
even when he had them at his mercy, and
silent before him, on a Sunday. He behaved
like a gentleman in this matter, where so
much temptation lurks, looking always at the
man whom he did not mean to hit, so that
the guilty one received it through him, and
felt himself better by comparison. In a word,
this parson did his duty well, and pleasantly
for all his flock; and nothing embittered
him, unless a man pretended to doctrine
without holy orders.

For the Doctor reasoned thus—and sound
it sounds—if divinity is a matter for Tom,
Dick, or Harry, how can there be degrees in
it? He held a degree in it, and felt what it had
cost; and not the parish only, but even his
own wife, was proud to have a doctor every
Sunday. And his wife took care that his rich
red hood, kerseymere small-clothes, and black
silk stockings upon calves of dignity, were
such that his congregation scorned the sur-
geons all the way to Beverley.

Happy in a pleasant nature, kindly heart,
and tranquil home, he was also happy in those

awards of life in which men are helpless. He
was blest with a good wife and three children,
doing well, and vigorous and hardy as the
air and clime and cliffs. His wife was not
quite of his own age, but old enough to understand and follow him faithfully down the
slope of years. A wife with mind enough to
know that a husband is not faultless, and
with heart enough to feel that if he were,
possibly she might not love him so. And
under her were comprised their children, two
boys at school, and a baby-girl at home.

So far, the rector of this parish was truly
blessed and blessing. But in every man's
lot must be some crook, since this crooked
world turned round. In Parson Upround's lot
the crook might seem a very small one; but
he found it almost too big for him. His
dignity, and peace of mind, large good-will
of ministry, and strong Christian sense of
magistracy, all were sadly pricked and
wounded by a very small thorn in the flesh of
his spirit.

Almost every honest man is the rightful
owner of a nick-name. When he was a boy
at school he could not do without one, and if
the other boys valued him, perhaps he had a

dozen. And afterwards, when there is less
perception of right and wrong and character,
in the weaker time of manhood, he may earn
another, if the spirit is within him.

But woe is him, if a nasty foe, or somebody
trying to be one, annoyed for the moment
with him, yet meaning no more harm than
pepper, smite him to the quick, at venture, in
his most retired and privy-conscienced hole.
And when this is done by a Non-conformist
to a Doctor of Divinity, and the man who.
does it owes some money to the man he does
it to, can the latter gentleman take a large
and genial view of his critic?

This gross wrong and ungrateful outrage
was inflicted thus. A leading Methodist from
Filey town, who owed the Doctor half-a-
guinea, came one summer and set up his staff
in the hollow of a limekiln, where he lived
upon fish for change of diet, and because he
could get it for nothing. This was a man of
some eloquence, and his calling in life was cob-
bling, and to encourage him therein, and keep
him from theology, the rector not only forgot
his half-guinea, but sent him three or four pairs
of riding-boots to mend, and let him charge his
own price, which was strictly heterodox. As

a part of the bargain, this fellow came to
church, and behaved as well as could be
hoped of a man who had received his money.
He sat by a pillar, and no more than crossed
his legs at the worst thing that disagreed with
him.　And it might have done him good, and
made a decent cobbler of him, if the parson
had only held him, when he got him on the
hook.　But this is the very thing which all
great preachers are too benevolent to do.　Dr.
Upround looked at this sinner, who was getting into a fright upon his own account,
though not a bad preacher when he could
afford it; and the cobbler could no more look
up at the Doctor, than when he charged him
a full crown beyond the contract.　In his
kindness for all who seemed convinced of
sin, the good preacher halted, and looked at
Mr. Jobbins with a soft, relaxing gaze.　Jobbins appeared as if he would come to
church for ever, and never cheat any sound
clergyman again; whereupon the generous
divine omitted a whole page of menaces prepared for him, and passed prematurely to the
tender strain, which always winds up a good
sermon.

Now what did Jobbins do in return for all

this magnanimous mercy? Invited to dine with the senior churchwarden upon the strength of having been at church, and to encourage him for another visit, and being asked, as soon as ever decency permitted, what he thought of Parson Upround's doctrine, between two crackles of young griskin (come straight from the rectory pig-sty), he was grieved to express a stern opinion long remembered at Flamborough,—

"Ca' yo yon mon 'Dr. Uproond'? I ca' un 'Dr. Upandoon.'"

From that day forth the rector of the parish was known far and wide as 'Dr. Upandown,' even among those who loved him best. For the name well described his benevolent practice of undoing any harsh thing he might have said, sometimes by a smile, and very often with a shilling, or a basket of spring cabbages. So that Mrs. Upround, when buttoning up his coat—which he always forgot to do for himself—did it with the words, "My dear, now scold no one; really it is becoming too expensive." "Shall I abandon duty," he would answer with some dignity, "while a shilling is sufficient to enforce it?"

Dr. Upround's people had now found out

that their minister and magistrate discharged
his duty towards his pillow, no less than to his
pulpit.   His parish had acquired, through the
work of generations, a habit of getting up at
night, and being all alive at cock-crow; and
the rector (while very new amongst them),
tried to bow—or rather rise—to night-
watch.   But a little of that exercise lasted
him for long; and he liked to talk of it afterwards; but for the present was obliged to
drop it.   For he found himself pale, when
his wife made him see himself; and his hours
of shaving were so dreadful; and scarcely a
bit of fair dinner could be got, with the whole
of the day thrown out so.   In short, he
settled it wisely, that the fishers of fish must
yield to the habits of fish, which cannot be
corrected; but the fishers of men (who can
live without catching them) need not be up
to all their hours, but may take them reason-
ably.

His parishioners—who could do very well
without him, so far as that goes, all the
week, and by no means wanted him among
their boats—joyfully left him to his own time
of day, and no more worried him out of season
than he worried them so.   It became a matter

of right feeling with them, not to ring a big bell, which the Rector had put up to challenge everybody's spiritual need, until the stable-clock behind the bell had struck ten, and finished gurgling.

For this reason, on St. Swithin's morn, in the said year 1782, the grannies, wives, and babes of Flamborough, who had been to help the launch, but could not pull the labouring oar, nor even hold the tiller, spent the time till ten o'clock in seeing to their own affairs—the most laudable of all pursuits for almost any woman. And then, with some little dispute among them (the offspring of the merest accident), they arrived in some force at the gate of Dr. Upround, and no woman liked to pull the bell, and still less to let another woman do it for her. But an old man came up who was quite deaf, and every one asked him to do it.

In spite of the scarcity of all good things, Mrs. Cockscroft had thoroughly fed the little stranger, and washed him, and undressed him, and set him up in her own bed, and wrapped him in her woollen shawl, because he shivered sadly; and there he stared about with wondering eyes, and gave great orders—so far as his new nurse could make out—but speaking

gibberish, as she said, and flying into a rage
because it was out of Christian knowledge.
But he seemed to understand some English,
although he could only pronounce two words,
both short, and in such conjunction quite un-
lawful for any except the highest Spiritual
Power. Mrs. Cockscroft, being a pious
woman, hoped that her ears were wrong, or
else that the words were foreign and meant
no harm, though the child seemed to take in
much of what was said, and when asked his
name, answered wrathfully, and as if everybody was bound to know — " Izunsabe,
Izunsabe! "

But now, when brought before Dr. Upround,
no child of the very best English stock could
look more calm and peaceful. He could walk
well enough, but liked better to be carried;
and the kind woman who had so taken him up,
was only too proud to carry him. Whatever
the rector and magistrate might say, her
meaning was to keep this little one, with her
husband's good consent, which she was sure
of getting.

" Set him down, ma'am, " the Doctor
said, when he had heard from half a dozen
good women all about him; " Mistress Cocks-

croft, put him on his legs, and let me question him."

But the child resisted this proceeding. With nature's inborn and just loathing of examination, he spun upon his little heels, and swore with all his might, at the same time throwing up his hands and twirling his thumbs in a very odd and foreign way.

"What a shocking child!" cried Mrs. Upround, who was come to know all about it. "Jane, run away with Miss Janetta."

"The child is not to blame," said the rector, "but only the people who have brought him up. A prettier or more clever little head I have never seen in all my life; and we studied such things at Cambridge. My fine little fellow, shake hands with me."

The boy broke off his vicious little dance, and looked up at this tall gentleman with great surprise. His dark eyes dwelt upon the parson's kindly face, with that power of inquiry which the very young possess, and then he put both little hands into the gentleman's, and burst into a torrent of the most heart-broken tears.

"Poor little man!" said the rector very gently, taking him up in his arms and patting

the silky black curls, while great drops fell,
and a nose was rubbed on his shoulder; "it is
early for you to begin bad times. Why, how
old are you, if you please?"

The little boy sat up on the kind man's
arm, and poked a small investigating finger
into the ear that was next to him, and the
locks just beginning to be marked with grey;
and then he said "Sore," and tossed his chin
up, evidently meaning—"make your best of
that." And the women drew a long breath,
and nudged at one another.

"Well done! Four years old, my dear.
You see that he understands English well
enough," said the parson to his parishioners;
" he will tell us all about himself by-and-by, if
we do not hurry him. You think him a French
child. I do not. Though the name which
he gives himself, "Izunsabe," has a French
aspect about it. Let me think. I will try
him with a French interrogation—"Parlez-
vous Français, mon enfant?"

Dr. Upround watched the effect of his
words with outward calm, but an inward
flutter. For if this clever child should reply
in French, the Doctor could never go on with
it, but must stand there before his congre-

gation, in a worse position than when he lost
his place, as sometimes happened, in a
sermon. With wild temerity he had given
vent to the only French words within his
knowledge; and he determined to follow them
up with Latin, if the worst came to the worst.

But luckily no harm came of this, but con-
trariwise, a lasting good. For the child
looked none the wiser, while the Doctor's
reputation was increased.

"Aha!" the good parson cried. "I was
sure that he was no Frenchman. But we
must hear something about him very soon,
for what you tell me is impossible. If he had
come from the sea, he must have been wet;
it could never be otherwise. Whereas, his
linen clothes are dry, and even quite lately
fullered—ironed you might call it."

"Please your worship," cried Mrs. Cockscroft, who was growing wild with jealousy;
"I did up all his little things, hours and
hours ere your hoose was up."

"Ah, you had night work! To be sure.
Were his clothes dry or wet, when you took
them off?"

"Not to say dry, your worship; and yet
not to say very wet. Betwixt and between,

like my good master's, when he cometh from
a pour of rain, or a heavy spray. And the
colour of the land was upon them here and
there. And the gold tags were sewn with
something wonderful. My best pair of scissors
would not touch it. I was frightened to put
them to the tub, your worship; but they up
and shone lovely like a tailor's buttons. My
master hath found him, sir ; and it lies with
him to keep him. And the Lord hath
taken away our Bob."

"It is true," said Dr. Upround gently, and
placing the child in her arms again, "the
Almighty has chastened you very sadly. This
child is not mine to dispose of, nor yours ; but
if he will comfort you, keep him till we hear
of him. I will take down in writing the parti-
culars of the case, when Captain Robin has
come home and had his rest, say at this
time to-morrow, or later; and then you will
sign them, and they shall be published. For
you know, Mrs. Cockscroft, however much
you may be taken with him, you must not
turn kidnapper. Moreover, it is needful, as
there may have been some wreck (though
none of you seem to have heard of any), that
this strange occurrence should be made

known. Then, if nothing is heard of it, you can keep him, and may the Lord bless him to you!"

Without any more ado, she kissed the child, and wanted to carry him straight away, after curtseying to his worship; but all the other women insisted on a smack of him, for pity's sake, and the pleasure of the gold, and to confirm the settlement. And a settlement it was; for nothing came of any publication of the case, such as in those days could be made without great expense and exertion.

So the boy grew up, tall, brave, and comely, and full of the spirit of adventure, as behoved a boy cast on the winds. So far as that goes, his foster-parents would rather have found him more steady and less comely; for if he must step into their lost son's shoes, he might do it, without seeming to outshine him. But they got over that little jealousy in time, when the boy began to be useful, and, so far as was possible, they kept him under, by quoting against him the character of Bob, bringing it back from heaven of a much higher quality then ever it was while beneath it. In vain did this living child aspire to such level; how can any earthly boy compare with one who never did a wrong thing, as soon as he was dead?

Passing that difficult question, and forbearing to compare a boy with angels, be he what he will, his first need (after that of victuals) is a name, whereby his fellow-boys may know him. Is he to be shouted at with— "Come here, what's your name"? or is he to be called (as if in high rebuke), "Boy"? And yet there are grown-up folk who do all this without hesitation, failing to remember their own predicament at a bygone period. Boys are as useful, in their way, as any other order; and if they can be said to do some mischief, they cannot be said to do it negligently. It is their privilege, and duty, to be truly active; and their Maker, having spread a dull world before them, has provided them with gifts of play, while their joints are supple.

The present boy, having been born without a father or a mother (so far as could yet be discovered), was driven to do what our ancestors must have done, when it was less needful. That is to say, to work his own name out, by some distinctive process. When the parson had clearly shown him not to be a Frenchman, a large contumely spread itself about, by reason of his gold, and eyes, and hair, and name (which might be meant for Isaak), that he was sprung from a race more honoured now than a hundred years ago. But the women declared that it could not be; and the rector desiring to christen him, because it might never have been done before, refused point-blank to put any " Isaac " in, and was satisfied with " Robin " only, the name of the man who had saved him.

The rector showed deep knowledge of his flock, which looked upon Jews as the goats of the Kingdom; for any Jew must die for a world of generations, ere ever a Christian thinks much of him. But finding him not to be a Jew, the other boys, instead of being satisfied, condemned him for a Dutchman.

Whatever he was, the boy throve well, and being so flouted by his play-mates, took to thoughts, and habits, and amusements of his own. Indoor life never suited him at all, nor too much of hard learning, although his capacity was such, that he took more advancement in an hour, than the thick heads of young Flamborough made in a whole leap-year of Sundays. For any Flamburian boy was considered a " Brain Scholar," and a

" Head - Languager," when he could write
down the parson's text, and chalk up a fish
on the weigh-board, so that his father or
mother could tell in three guesses what manner
of fish it was. And very few indeed had
ever passed this trial.

For young Robin it was a very hard thing to
be treated so by the other boys. He could run,
or jump, or throw a stone, or climb a rock
with the best of them; but all these things
he must do by himself, simply because he
had no name. A feeble youth would have
moped; but Robin only grew more resolute.
Alone he did what the other boys would
scarcely in competition dare. No crag was
too steep for him, no cave too dangerous
and wave-beaten, no race of the tide so strong
and swirling as to scare him of his wits. He
seemed to rejoice in danger, having very
little else to rejoice in; and he won for himself by nimble ways and rapid turns on land
and sea, the name of " Lithe," or " Lyth,"
and made it famous even far inland.

For it may be supposed that his love of
excitement, versatility, and daring, demanded
a livelier outlet than the slow toil of deep-
sea fishing. To the most patient, persevering,

and long-suffering of the arts, Robin Lyth did not take kindly, although he was so handy with a boat. Old Robin vainly strove to cast his angling mantle over him. The gifts of the youth were brighter and higher; he showed an inborn fitness for the lofty development of free-trade. Eminent powers must force their way, as now they were doing with Napoleon; and they did the same with Robin Lyth, without exacting tithe in kind of all the foremost human race.

CHAPTER XII.

IN A LANE, NOT ALONE.

STEPHEN ANERLEY's daughter was by no means of a crooked mind, but open as the day in all things, unless any one mistrusted her, and showed it by cross-questioning. When this was done, she resented it quickly, by concealing the very things which she would have told of her own accord; and it so happened that the person to whom of all she should have been most open, was the one most apt to check her by suspicious curiosity. And now her mother already began to do this, as concerned the smuggler, knowing from the revenue-officer that her Mary must have seen him. Mary, being a truthful damsel, told no lies about it; but, on the other hand, she did not rush forth with all the history, as she probably would have done, if left unexamined.

And so she said nothing about the ear-ring,
or the run that was to come off that week, or
the riding-skirt, or a host of little things, including her promise to visit Bempton Lane.

On the other hand, she had a mind to tell
her father, and take his opinion about it all.
But he was a little cross that evening, not
with her, but with the world at large; and
that discouraged her; and then she thought
that being an officer of the king—as he liked
to call himself sometimes—he might feel
bound to give information about the impending process of free-trade; which to her
would be a breach of honour, considering how
she knew of it.

Upon the whole, she heartily wished that
she never had seen that Robin Lyth; and then
she became ashamed of herself, for indulging
such a selfish wish. For he might have been
lying dead, but for her; and then what would
become of the many poor people, whose
greatest comfort he was said to be? And
what good could arise from his destruction,
if cruel officers compassed it? Free-trade
must be carried on, for the sake of everybody, including Captain Carroway himself;
and if an old and ugly man succeeded a young

and generous one, as leader of the free-trade movement, all the women of the county would put the blame on her.

Looking at these things loftily, and with a strong determination not to think twice of what any one might say who did not understand the subject, Mary was forced at last to the stern conclusion that she must keep her promise. Not only because it was a promise —although that went a very long way with her—but also because there seemed no other chance of performing a positive duty. Simple honesty demanded that she should restore to the owner a valuable, and beyond all doubt important, piece of property. Two hours had she spent in looking for it, and deprived her dear father of his breakfast-shrimps ; and was all this trouble to be thrown away, and herself perhaps accused of theft, because her mother was so short and sharp in wanting to know everything, and to turn it her own way ?

The trinket which she had found at last seemed to be a very uncommon and precious piece of jewelry; it was made of pure gold minutely chased and threaded with curious workmanship, in form like a melon, and bear-

ing what seemed to be characters of some
foreign language; there might be a spell, or
even witchcraft in it, and the sooner it was out
of her keeping the better. Nevertheless she
took very good care of it, wrapping it in
lamb's wool, and peeping at it many times a
day, to be sure that it was safe. Until it
made her think of the owner so much, and
the many wonders she had heard about him,
that she grew quite angry with herself and
it, and locked it away, and then looked at it
again.

As luck would have it, on the very day when
Mary was to stroll down Bempton Lane (not
to meet any one, of course, but simply for the
merest chance of what might happen), her
father had business at Driffield corn-market,
which would keep him from home nearly all the
day. When his daughter heard of it, she was
much cast down; for she hoped that he might
have been looking about on the northern part
of the farm, as he generally was in the afternoon; and although he could not see Bempton Lane at all, perhaps, without some newly
acquired power of seeing round sharp corners, still it would have been a comfort and a
strong resource for conscience, to have felt

that he was not so very far away.   And this
feeling of want made his daughter resolve to
have some one at any rate near her.   If Jack
had only been at home, she need have
sought no further, for he would have entered
into all her thoughts about it, and obeyed her
orders beautifully.   But Willie was quite
different, and hated any trouble, being spoiled
so by his mother, and the maidens all around
them.

However, in such a strait, what was
there to do, but to trust in Willie, who was
old enough, being five years in front of Mary,
and then to try to make him sensible ? Willie Anerley had no idea that anybody—far
less his own sister—could take such a view of
him.   He knew himself to be, and all would
say the same of him, superior in his original
gifts, and his manner of making use of them,
to the rest of the family put together.   He
had spent a month in Glasgow, when the
whole place was astir with the ferment of
many great inventions, and another month in
Edinburgh, when that noble city was a-glow
with the dawn of large ideas; also, he had
visited London, foremost of his family, and
seen enough of new things there to fill all

Yorkshire with surprise; and the result of such wide experience was that he did not like hard work at all. Neither could he even be content to accept and enjoy, without labour of his own, the many good things provided for him. He was always trying to discover something, which never seemed to answer, and continually flying after something new, of which he never got fast hold. In a word, he was spoiled, by nature first, and then by circumstances, for the peaceful life of his ancestors, and the unacknowledged blessings of a farmer.

"Willie, dear, will you come with me?" Mary said to him that day, catching him as he ran down stairs, to air some inspiration; "Will you come with me for just one hour? I wish you would; and I would be so thankful."

"Child, it is quite impossible;" he answered, with a frown which set off his delicate eyebrows, and high but rather narrow forehead; "you always want me at the very moment when I have the most important work in hand. Any childish whim of yours matters more than hours and hours of hard labour."

"Oh, Willie, but you know how I try to

help you, and all the patterns I cut out last week! Do come for once, Willie; if you refuse, you will never, never forgive yourself."

Willie Anerley was as goodnatured as any self-indulgent youth can be; he loved his sister in his way, and was indebted to her for getting out of a great many little scrapes. He saw how much she was in earnest now, and felt some desire to know what it was about. Moreover—which settled the point— he was getting tired of sticking to one thing for a time unusually long with him. But he would not throw away the chance of scoring a huge debt of gratitude.

"Well, do what you like with me," he answered, with a smile; "I never can have my own way five minutes. It serves me quite right for being so goodnatured."

Mary gave him a kiss, which must have been an object of ambition to anybody else; but it only made him wipe his mouth; and presently the two set forth upon the path towards Bempton.

Robin Lyth had chosen well his place for meeting Mary. The lane (of which he knew every yard, as well as he knew the rocks themselves) was deep, and winding, and

fringed with bushes, so that an active and
keen-eyed man might leap into thicket, almost
before there was a fair chance of shooting
him. He knew well enough that he might
trust Mary; but he never could be sure that
the bold " coast-riders," despairing by this
time of catching him at sea, and longing for
the weight of gold put upon his head, might
not be setting privy snares to catch him in his
walks abroad. They had done so when they
pursued him up the Dyke; and though he
was inclined to doubt the strict legality of
that proceeding, he could not see his way to
a fair discussion of it, in case of their putting
a bullet through him. And this consideration made him careful.

The brother and sister went on well by the
footpath over the uplands of the farm, and
crossing the neck of the Flamburn peninsula,
tripped away merrily northward. The wheat
looked healthy, and the barley also, and a
four-acre patch of potatoes smelled sweetly
(for the breeze of them was pleasant in their
wholesome days), and Willie, having over-
worked his brain, according to his own account of it, strode along loftily before his
sister, casting over his shoulder an eddy of

some large ideas, with which he had been
visited, before she interrupted him. But, as
nothing ever came of them, they need not
here be stated. From a practical point of
view, however, as they both had to live upon
the profits of the farm, it pleased them to observe what a difference there was, when they
had surmounted the chine, and began to de-
scend towards the north upon other people's
land. Here all was damp and cold and slow;
and chalk looked slimy instead of being clean;
and shadowy places had an oozy cast; and trees
(wherever they could stand) were facing the
east with wrinkled visage, and the west with
wiry beards. Willie (who had, among other
great inventions, a scheme for improvement of
the climate) was reminded at once of all
the things he meant to do in that way; and
making, as he always did, a great point of
getting observations first—a point whereon
he stuck fast mainly—without any time for
delay he applied himself to a rapid study of
the subject. He found some things just like
other things which he had seen in Scotland,
yet differing so as to prove more clearly, than
even their resemblance did, the value of his
discovery.

"Look!" he cried, "can anything be clearer? The cause of all these evils is, not (as an ignorant person might suppose) the want of sunshine, or too much wet, but an inadequate movement of the air—"

"Why, I thought it was always blowing up here! The very last time I came, my bonnet-strings were split."

"You do not understand me; you never do. When I say inadequate, I mean of course incorrect, inaccurate, unequable. Now the air is a fluid; you may stare as you like, Mary, but the air has been proved to be a fluid. Very well, no fluid in large bodies moves with an equal velocity throughout. Part of it is rapid, and part quite stagnant. The stagnant places of the air produce this green scum, this mossy, unwholesome, and injurious stuff; while the over-rapid motion causes this iron appearance, this hard surface, and general sterility. By the simplest of simple contrivances, I make this evil its own remedy. An equable impulse given to the air produces an adequate uniform flow, preventing stagnation in one place, and excessive vehemence in another. And the beauty of it is, that by my new invention I make the air itself correct and regulate its own inequalities."

"How clever you are to be sure!" exclaimed Mary, wondering that her father could not see it. "Oh, Willie, you will make your fortune by it! However do you do it?"

"The simplicity of it is such that even you can understand it. All great discoveries are simple. I fix in a prominent situation a large and vertically revolving fan, of a light and vibrating substance. The movement of the air causes this to rotate, by the mere force of the impact. The rotation and the vibration of the fan convert an irregular impulse into a steady and equable undulation; and such is the elasticity of the fluid called, in popular language, ' the air,' that for miles around the rotation of this fan regulates the circulation, modifies extremes, annihilates sterility, and makes it quite impossible for moss and green scum, and all this sour growth to live. Even you can see, Mary, how beautiful it is."

"Yes, that I can!" she answered simply, as they turned the corner upon a large windmill, with arms revolving merrily; "but, Willie, dear, would not Farmer Topping's mill, perpetually going as it is, answer the same purpose? And yet the moss seems to be as thick as ever here, and the ground as naked!"

"Tush!" cried Willie. "Stuff and non-sense! When will you girls understand? Good-bye! I will throw away no more time on you."

Without stopping to finish his sentence he was off, and out of sight both of the mill and Mary, before the poor girl, who had not the least intention of offending him, could even beg his pardon, or say how much she wanted him; for she had not dared as yet to tell him what was the purpose of her walk, his nature being such that no one, not even his own mother, could tell what conclusion he might come to upon any practical question. He might rush off at once to put the Revenue-men on the smuggler's track; or he might stop his sister from going; or he might (in the absence of his father) order a feast to be pre-pared, and fetch the outlaw to be his guest. So Mary had resolved not to tell him until the last moment, when he could do none of these things.

But now she must either go on all alone, or

give up her purpose and break her promise. After some hesitation she determined to go on, for the place would scarcely seem so very lonely now with the windmill in view, which would always remind her henceforth of her dear brother William. It was perfectly certain that Captain Robin Lyth, whose fame for chivalry was everywhere, and whose character was all in all to him with the ladies who bought his silks and lace, would see her through all danger caused by confidence in him; and really it was too bad of her to admit any paltry misgivings. But, reason as she might, her young conscience told her that this was not the proper thing for her to do; and she made up her mind not to do it again. Then she laughed at the notion of being ever even asked, and told herself that she was too conceited; and to cut the matter short, went very bravely down the hill.

The lane, which came winding from the beach up to the windmill, was as pretty a lane as may anywhere be found in any other county than that of Devon. With a Devonshire lane it could not presume to vie, having little of the glorious garniture of fern, and nothing of the crystal brook that leaps at

every corner; no arches of tall ash, keyed
with dog-rose, and not much of honey-suckle,
and a sight of other wants which people feel
who have lived in the plenitude of everything.
But, in spite of all that, the lane was very fine
for Yorkshire.

On the other hand, Mary had prettier ankles,
and a more graceful and lighter walk than the
Devonshire lanes, which like to echo something, for the most part seem accustomed to;
and the short dress of the time made good
such favourable facts when found. Nor was
this all that could be said, for the maiden
(while her mother was so busy pickling cab-
bage, from which she drove all intruders)
had managed to forget what the day of the
week was, and had opened the drawer that
should be locked up until Sunday. To walk
with such a handsome tall fellow as Willie,
compelled her to look like something too; and
without any thought of it she put her best
hat on, and a very pretty thing with some
French name, and made of a delicate peach-
coloured silk, which came down over her
bosom, and tied in the neatest of knots at the
small of her back, which at that time of life
was very small. All these were the gifts of

her dear Uncle Popplewell, upon the other side of Filey, who might have been married for forty years, but nobody knew how long it was, because he had no children, and so he made Mary his darling. And this ancient gentleman had leanings towards free trade.

Whether these goods were French or not—which no decent person could think of asking—no French damsel could have put them on better, or shown a more pleasing appearance in them; for Mary's desire was to please all people who meant no harm to her—as nobody could—and yet to let them know that her object was only to do what was right, and to never think of asking whether she looked this, that, or the other. Her mother, as a matter of duty, told her how plain she was almost every day; but the girl was not of that opinion; and when Mrs. Anerley finished her lecture (as she did nine times in ten) by turning the glass to the wall, and declaring that beauty was a snare skin-deep, with a frown of warning instead of a smile of comfort, then Mary believed in her looking-glass again, and had the smile of comfort on her own face.

However, she never thought of that just

now, but only of how she could do her duty,
and have no trouble in her own mind with
thinking, and satisfy her father when she told
him all, as she meant to do, when there could
be no harm done to any one; and this, as she
heartily hoped, would be to-morrow. And
truly, if there did exist any vanity at all, it
was not confined to the sex in which it is so
much more natural and comely.

For when a very active figure came to light
suddenly, at a little elbow of the lane, and
with quick steps advanced towards Mary, she
was lost in surprise at the gaiety, not to say
grandeur, of its apparel. A broad hat, looped
at the side, and having a pointed black crown,
with a scarlet feather, and a dove-coloured
brim, sat well upon the mass of crisp black
curls. A short blue jacket of the finest
Flemish cloth, and set (not too thickly) with
embossed silver buttons, left properly open
the strong brown neck, while a shirt of pale
blue silk, with a turned-down collar of fine
needlework, fitted, without a wrinkle or a
pucker, the broad and amply rounded chest.
Then a belt of brown leather, with an anchor
clasp, and empty loops for either fire-arm or
steel, supported true sailor's trousers of the

purest white and the noblest man-of-war cut;
and where these widened at the instep shone
a lovely pair of pumps, with buckles radiant
of best Bristol diamonds.   The wearer of all
these splendours smiled, and seemed to become them as they became him.

"Well," thought Mary, "how free trade
must pay! What a pity that he is not in the
Royal Navy!"

With his usual quickness, and the self-
esteem which added such lustre to his character, the smuggler perceived what was passing
in her mind, but he was not rude enough to
say so.

"Young lady," he began—and Mary, with
all her wisdom, could not help being fond of
that; "young lady, I was quite sure that you
would keep your word."

"I never do anything else," she answered,
showing that she scarcely looked at him; "I
have found this for you, and then good-
bye."

"Surely you will wait to hear my thanks,
and to know what made me dare to ask you,
after all you had done for me already, to
begin again for me.   But I am such an outcast that I never should have done it."

"I never saw any one look more thoroughly unlike an outcast," Mary said; and then she was angry with herself, for speaking, and glancing, and worst of all for smiling.

"Ladies who live on land can never underderstand what we go through," Robin replied in his softest voice, as rich as the murmur of the summer sea; "when we expect great honours, we try to look a little tidy, as any one but a common boor would do; and we laugh at ourselves for trying to look well after all the knocking about we get. Our time is short—we must make the most of it."

"Oh, please not to talk in such a dreadful way;" said Mary.

"You remind me of my dear friend Dr. Upround, the very best man in the whole world, I believe. He always says to me, 'Robin, Robin—'"

"What, is Dr. Upandown a friend of yours?" Mary exclaimed in amazement, and with a stoppage of the foot that was poised for quick departure.

"Dr. Upandown, as many people call him," said the smuggler, with a tone of condemnation, "is the best and dearest friend I have, next to Captain and Mistress Cockscroft, who may have been heard of at Anerley Manor. Dr. Upround is our magistrate and clergyman, and he lets people say what they like against me, while he honours me with his friendship. I must not stay long, to thank you even, because I am going to the dear old doctor's, for supper at seven o'clock, and a game of chess."

"Oh dear, oh dear! And he is such a Justice; and yet they shot at you last week! It makes me wonder when I hear such things."

"Young lady, it makes everybody wonder. In my opinion. there never could be a more shameful murder than to shoot me; and yet but for you, it would surely have been done."

"You must not dwell upon such things," said Mary; "they may have a very bad effect upon your mind. But good-bye, Captain Lyth; I forgot that I was robbing Dr. Upround of your society."

"Shall I be so ungrateful as not to see you safe upon your own land, after all your trouble? My road to Flamborough lies that way. Surely you will not refuse to hear what

made me so anxious about this bauble, which
now will be worth ten times as much. I
never saw it look so bright before."

"It—it must be the sand has made it
shine," the maiden stammered, with a fine
bright blush; "it does the same to my
shrimping-net."

"Ah, shrimping is a very fine pursuit!
There is nothing I love better; what pools I
could show you, if I only might; pools where
you may fill a sack with large prawns in a
single tide—pools known to nobody but myself. When do you think of going shrimping
next?"

"Perhaps next summer I may try again,
if Captain Carroway will come with me."

"That is too unkind of you. How very
harsh you are to me!. I could hardly have
believed it, after all that you have done. And
you really do not care to hear the story of
this relic?"

"If I could stop, I should like it very much.
But my brother, who came with me, may
perhaps be waiting for me." Mary knew
that this was not very likely; still it was just
possible, for Willie's ill-tempers seldom lasted
very long; and she wanted to let the smug-

gler know that she had not come all alone to meet him.

"I shall not be two minutes," Robin Lyth replied; "I have been forced to learn short talking. May I tell you about this trinket?"

"Yes, if you will only begin at once, and finish by the time we get to that corner."

"That is very short measure for a tale," said Robin, though he liked her all the better for such qualities; "however, I will try; only walk a little slower. Nobody knows where I was born, any more than they know how or why. Only when I came upon this coast as a very little boy, and without knowing anything about it, they say that I had very wonderful buttons of gold upon a linen dress, adorned with gold lace, which I used to wear on Sundays. Dr. Upround ordered them to keep those buttons, and was to have had them in his own care; but, before that, all of them were lost save two. My parents, as I call them from their wonderful goodness, kinder than the ones who have turned me on the world (unless themselves went out of it), resolved to have my white coat done up grandly, when I grew too big for it, and to lay it by in lavender; and knowing of a great

man in the gold-lace trade, as far away as
Scarborough, they sent it by a fishing-smack
to him, with people whom they knew
thoroughly. That was the last of it ever
known here. The man swore a manifest
that he never saw it, and threatened them
with libel; and the smack was condemned,
and all her hands impressed, because of some
trifle she happened to carry; and nobody
knows any more of it. But two of the buttons had fallen off, and good mother had put
them by, to give a last finish to the coat herself; and when I grew up and had to go to
sea at night, they were turned into a pair of
ear-rings. There, now, Miss Anerley, I have
not been long, and you know all about it."

"How very very lonesome it must be for
you," said Mary with a gentle gaze, which,
coming from such lovely eyes, went straight
into his heart, "to have no one belonging to
you by right, and to seem to belong to nobody.
I am sure I cannot tell what ever I should do,
without any father, or mother, or uncle, or
even a cousin to be certain of."

"All the ladies seem to think that it is
rather hard upon me," Robin answered, with
an excellent effort at a sigh; "but I do my

very best to get on without them. And one thing that helps me most of all is when kind ladies, who have good hearts, allow me to talk to them as if I had a sister. This makes me forget what I am sometimes."

"You never should try to forget what you are. Everybody in the world speaks well of you. Even that cruel Lieutenant Carroway cannot help admiring you. And if you have taken to free-trade, what else could you do, when you had no friends, and even your coat was stolen?"

"High-minded people take that view of it, I know. But I do not pretend to any such excuse. I took to free-trade for the sake of my friends—to support the old couple who have been so good to me."

"That is better still; it shows such good principle. My Uncle Popplewell has studied the subject of what they call 'political economy,' and he says that the country requires free-trade, and the only way to get it is to go on so that the Government must give way at last. However, I need not instruct you about that; and you must not stop any longer."

"Miss Anerley, I will not encroach upon your kindness. You have said things that I never shall forget. On the continent I meet very many ladies who tell me good things, and make me better; but not at all as you have done. A minute of talk with you is worth an hour with anybody else. But I fear that you laugh at me all the while, and are only too glad to be rid of me. Good-bye. May I kiss your hand? God bless you!"

Mary had no time to say a single word, or even to express her ideas by a look, before Robin Lyth, with all his bright apparel, was "conspicuous by his absence." As a diving bird disappears from a gun, or a trout from a shadow on his hover, or even a debtor from his creditor, so the great free-trader had vanished into lightsome air, and left emptiness behind him.

The young maid, having been prepared to yield him a few yards more of good advice, if he held out for another corner, now could only say to herself that she never had met such a wonderful man. So active, strong, and astonishingly brave; so thoroughly acquainted with foreign lands, yet superior to their ladies; so able to see all the meaning of good words, and to value them when offered quietly; so sweet in his manner, and voice, and looks; and with all his fame so unpretending; and—much as it frightened her to think it—really seeming to be afraid of her.

CHAPTER XIII.

GRUMBLING AND GROWLING.

WHILE these successful runs went on, and great authorities smiled at seeing the little authorities set at nought, and men of the revenue smote their breasts for not being born good smugglers, and the general public was well-pleased, and congratulated them cordially upon their accomplishment of nought, one man there was whose noble spirit chafed and knew no comfort. He strode up and down at Coast-guard Point, and communed with himself, while Robin held sweet converse in the lane.

"Why was I born?" the sad Carroway cried; "why was I thoroughly educated, and trained in both services of the king, expected to rise, and beginning to rise, till a vile bit of splinter stopped me; and then sent down to this hole of a place to starve, and be laughed at, and baffled by a boy? Another lucky run, and the revenue bamboozled, and the whole of us sent upon a wild-goose chase! Every gapper-mouth zany grinning at me, and scoundrels swearing that I get my share! And the only time I have had my dinner with my knees crook'd, for at least a fortnight, was at Anerley Farm on Sunday. I am not sure that even they wouldn't turn against me; I am certain that pretty girl would. I've a great mind to throw it up— a great mind to throw it up. It is hardly the work for a gentleman born, and the grandson of a rear-admiral. Tinkers' and tailors' sons get the luck now; and a man of good blood is put on the back-shelf, behind the blacking-bottles. A man who has battled for his country—"

"Charles, are you coming to your dinner, once more?"

"No, I am not. There's no dinner worth coming to. You and the children may eat the rat-pie. A man who has battled for his country, and bled till all his veins were empty, and it took two men to hold him up, and yet waved his sword at the head of them,

—it is the downright contradiction of the world in everything, for him to poke about with pots and tubs, like a pig in a brewery, grain-hunting."

"Once more, Charles, there is next to nothing left. The children are eating for their very lives. If you stay out there another minute, you must take the consequence."

"Alas, that I should combine capacity with incapability! My dear, put a little bit under a basin, if any of them has no appetite. I wanted just to think a little."

"Charles, they have all got tremendous appetites. It is the way the wind is. You may think by-and-by; but if you want to eat, you must do it now, or never."

"'Never' never suits me in that matter," the brave lieutenant answered; "Matilda, put Geraldine to warm the pewter plate for me. Geraldine, darling, you can do it with your mouth full."

The commander of the coast-guard turned abruptly from his long indignant stride, and entered the cottage provided for him, and which he had peopled so speedily.

Small as it was, it looked beautifully clean

and neat; and everybody used to wonder how
Mrs. Carroway kept it so.   But in spite of all
her troubles and many complaints, she was
very proud of this little house, with its
healthful position, and beautiful outlook over
the bay of Bridlington.   It stood in a niche
of the low soft cliff, where now the sea-parade
extends from the northern pier of Bridlington Quay; and when the roadstead between
that and the point was filled with a fleet of
every kind of craft, or better still when they
all made sail at once—as happened when a
trusty breeze arose—the view was lively, and
very pleasant, and full of moving interest.
Often one of his Majesty's cutters, "Sword-
fish," "Kestrel," or "Albatross" would swoop
in with all sail set, and hover, while the
skipper came ashore to see the "Ancient
Carroway," as this vigilant officer was called;
and sometimes even a sloop of war, armed
brigantine, or light corvette, prowling for
recruits, or cruising for their training,
would run in under the Head, and overhaul
every wind-bound ship with a very high
hand.

"Ancient   Carroway,"—as   old   friends
called him, and even young people who had

never seen him,—was famous upon this coast
now, for nearly three degrees of latitude.
He had dwelled here long, and in highly
good content, hospitably treated by his neighbours, and himself more hospitable than his
wife could wish. Until two troubles in his
life arose, and from year to year grew worse
and worse. One of these troubles was the
growth of mouths, in number and size, that
required to be filled; and the other trouble
was the rampant growth of smuggling, and
the glory of that upstart Robin Lyth. Now
let it be lawful to take that subject first.

Fair Robin, though not at all anxious for
fame, but modestly willing to decline it, had
not been successful—though he worked so
much by night—in preserving sweet obscurity.
His character was public, and set on high by
fortune, to be gazed at from wholly different
points of view. From their narrow and lime-
eyed outlook the coast-guard beheld in him
the latest incarnation of Old Nick; yet they
hated him only in an abstract manner, and
as men feel towards that evil one. Magistrates also, and the large protective powers,
were arrayed against him, yet happy to
abstain from laying hands, when their hands

were their own, upon him. And many of the farmers, who should have been his warmest friends, and best customers, were now so attached to their king and country, by bellicose warmth and army-contracts, that instead of a guinea for a four-gallon anker, they would offer three crowns, or the exciseman. And not only conscience, but short cash, after three bad harvests, constrained them.

Yet the staple of public opinion was sound, as it must be where women predominate. The best of women could not see why they should not have anything they wanted, for less than it cost the maker. To gaze at a sister woman better dressed, at half the money, was simply to abjure every lofty principle. And to go to church with a counterfeit on, when the genuine lace was in the next pew, on a body of inferior standing, was a downright outrage to the congregation, the rector, and all religion. A cold-blooded creature, with no pin-money, might reconcile it with her principles, if any she had, to stand up like a dowdy, and allow a poor man to risk his life, by shot and storm and starvation, and then to deny him a word or a look, because of his coming with the

genuine thing, at a quarter the price fat tradesmen asked, who never stirred out of their
shops when it rained, for a thing that was a
story and an imposition. Charity, duty, and
common honesty to their good husbands, in
these bad times, compelled them to make the
very best of bargains; of which they got really
more and more, as those brave mariners
themselves bore witness, because of the
depression in the free-trade now, and the
glorious victories of England. Were they
bound to pay three times the genuine value,
and then look a figure, and be laughed at?

And as for Captain Carroway, let him scold,
and threaten, and stride about, and be
jealous, because his wife dare not buy true
things, poor creature—although there were
two stories also about that, and the quanti-
ties of things that he got for nothing, whenever he was clever enough to catch them, which
scarcely ever happened, thank goodness! Let
Captain Carroway attend to his own business;
unless he was much belied, he had a wife
who would keep him to it. Who was Captain
Carroway to come down here, without even
being born in Yorkshire, and lay down the
law, as if he owned the manor?

Lieutenant Carroway had heard such questions, but disdained to answer them. He knew who he was, and what his grandfather had been, and he never cared a—short word, what sort of stuff long tongues might prate of him. Barbarous broad-drawlers, murderers of his Majesty's English, could they even pronounce the name of an officer highly distinguished for many years in both of the royal services? That was his description, and the Yorkshire yokels might go and read it— if read they could—in the pages of authority.

Like the celebrated calf that sucked two cows, Carroway had drawn royal pay, though in very small drains, upon either element, beginning with a skeleton regiment, and then, when he became too hot for it, diving off into a frigate, as a recommended volunteer. Here he was more at home, though he never ceased longing to be a general; and having the credit of fighting well ashore, he was looked at with interest when he fought a fight at sea. He fought it uncommonly well, and it was good, and so many men fell that he picked up his commission, and got into a fifty-two gun ship. After several years of service, without promotion, for his grand-

father's name was worn out now, and the
wars were not properly constant, there came
a very lively succession of fights, and Carroway got into all of them, or at least into all
the best of them. And he ought to have
gone up much faster than he did, and he must
have done so but for his long lean jaws, the
which are the worst things that any man can
have. Not only because of their own con-
sumption, and slow length of leverage, but
mainly on account of the sadness they impart,
and the timid recollection of a hungry wolf,
to the man who might have lifted up a fatter
individual.

But in Rodney's great encounter with
the Spanish fleet, Carroway showed such a
dauntless spirit, and received such a wound,
that it was impossible not to pay him some
attention. His name was near the bottom of
a very long list, but it made a mark on some
one's memory, depositing a chance of coming
up some day, when he should be reported hit
again. And so good was his luck, that he
soon was hit again, and a very bad hit it was;
but still he got over it without promotion,
because that enterprise was one in which
nearly all our men ran away, and therefore

required to be well pushed up, for the sake of
the national honour. When such things
happen, the few who stay behind must be
left behind in the "Gazette" as well. That
wound, therefore, seemed at first to go against
him, but he bandaged it, and plastered it,
and hoped for better luck. And his third
wound truly was a blessed one, a slight one,
and taken in the proper course of things,
without a slur upon any of his comrades.
This set him up again with advancement
and appointment, and enabled him to marry
and have children seven.

The lieutenant was now about fifty years
of age, gallant and lively as ever, and resolute
to attend to his duty and himself as well.
His duty was now alongshore, in command
of the Coast-guard of the East District; for
the loss of a good deal of one heel made it
hard for him to step about as he should do
when afloat. The place suited him, and he
was fond of it, although he grumbled sometimes about his grandfather, and went on as
if his office was beneath him. He abused all
his men, and all the good ones liked him, and
respected him for his clear English. And
he enjoyed this free exercise of language out

of doors, because inside his threshold he was
on his P's and Q's. To call him "ugly
Carroway," as coarse people did, because of
a scar across his long bold nose, was petty
and unjust, and directly contradicted by his
own and his wife's opinion. For nobody
could have brighter eyes, or a kindlier smile,
and more open aspect in the forepart of
the week, while his Sunday shave retained
its influence, so far as its limited area went,
for he kept a long beard always. By Wed-
nesday he certainly began to look grim, and
on Saturday ferocious, pending the advent of
the Bridlington barber, who shaved all the
Quay every Sunday. But his mind was none
the worse, and his daughters liked him better,
when he rasped their young cheeks with his
beard, and paid a penny. For to his children he
was a most loving and tender-hearted father,
puzzled at their number, and sometimes
perplexed at having to feed and clothe them,
yet happy to give them his last and go without, and even ready to welcome more, if
Heaven should be pleased to send them.

But Mrs. Carroway, most fidgety of women,
and born of a well-shorn family, was unhappy from the middle to the end of the

week that she could not scrub her husband's beard off. This lady's sense of human crime, and of everything hateful in creation, expressed itself mainly in the word "dirt." Her rancour against that nobly tranquil, and most natural of elements, inured itself into a downright passion. From babyhood she had been notorious for kicking her little legs out, at the least speck of dust upon a tiny red shoe. Her father, a clergyman, heard so much of this, and had so many children of a different stamp, that when he came to christen her, at six months of age (which used to be considered quite an early time of life) he put upon her the name of "Lauta," to which she thoroughly acted up; but people having ignorance of foreign tongues, said that he always meant "Matilda."

Such was her nature, and it grew upon her; so that when a young and gallant officer, tall and fresh, and as clean as a frigate, was captured by her neat bright eyes, very clean run, and sharp cut-water, she began to like to look at him. Before very long, his spruce trim ducks, careful scrape of Brunswick-leather boots, clean pocket-handkerchiefs, and fine specklessness, were making and keeping a well-swept path to the thoroughly-dusted store-room of her heart. How little she dreamed, in those virgin days, that the future could ever contain a week when her Charles would decline to shave more than once, and then have it done for him on a Sunday!

She hesitated, for she had her thoughts — doubts she disdained to call them—but still he forgot once to draw his boots sideways after having purged the toe and heel, across the bristle of her father's mat. With the quick eye of love, he perceived her frown, and the very next day he conquered her. His scheme was unworthy, as it substituted corporate for personal purity; still it succeeded, as unworthy schemes will do. On the birthday of his sacred Majesty, Charles took Matilda to see his ship, the 48-gun frigate "Immaculate," commanded by a well-known martinet. Her spirit fell within her, like the Queen of Sheba's, as she gazed, but trembled to set down foot upon the trim order and the dazzling choring. She might have survived the strict purity of all things, the deck-lines whiter than Parian marble, the bulwarks brighter than the cheek-piece of a grate, the breeches of the guns like goodly gold, and not a whisker of a rope's end curling the wrong way; if only she could have espied a swab, or a bucket, or a flake of holystone, or any indicament of labour done. "Artis est celare artem;" this art was unfathomable.

Matilda was fain to assure herself that the main part of this might be superficial, like a dish-cover polished with the spots on, and she lost her handkerchief on purpose to come back and try a little test-work of her own. This was a piece of unstopped knotting in the panel of a hatchway, a resinous hole that must catch and keep any speck of dust meandering on the wayward will of wind. Her cambric came out as white as it went in !

She surrendered at discretion, and became the prize of Carroway.

Now people at Bridlington Quay declared that the lieutenant, though he might have carried off a prize, was certainly not the prize-master; and they even went so far as to say that "he could scarcely call his soul his own." The matter was no concern of theirs, neither were their conclusions true. In little things the gallant officer, for the sake of discipline and peace, submitted to due authority, and being so much from home, he left all household matters to a firm control. In return for this, he was always thought of first, and the best of everything was kept for him, and Mrs. Carroway quoted him to others as a wonder, though she may not have done so to himself. And so, upon the whole, they got on very well together.

Now on this day, when the lieutenant had exhausted a grumble of unusual intensity, and the fair Geraldine (his eldest child) had obeyed him to the letter, by keeping her mouth full, while she warmed a plate for him, it was not long before his usual luck befell the bold Carroway. Rap, rap, came a knock at the side-door of his cottage, a knock only too familiar; and he heard the gruff voice of Cadman—" Can I see his Honour immediately?"

" No, you cannot," replied Mrs. Carroway. " One would think you were all in a league to starve him. No sooner does he get half a mouthful—"

" Geraldine, put it on the hob, my dear, and a basin over it. Matilda, my love, you know my maxim—' Duty first, dinner afterwards.' Cadman, I will come with you."

The revenue-officer took up his hat (which

had less time now than his plate to get
cold) and followed Cadman to the usual place
for holding privy councils. This was under
the heel of the pier (which was then about half
as long as now) at a spot where the outer wall
combed over, to break the crest of the surges
in the height of a heavy eastern gale. At
neap tides, and in moderate weather, this
place was dry, with a fine salt smell, and with
nothing in front of it but the sea, and nothing
behind it but solid stone wall, any one would
think that here must be commune sacred,
secret, and secluded from eavesdroppers.
And yet it was not so, by reason of a very
simple reason.

Upon the roadway of the pier, and over
against a mooring-post, where the parapet
and the pier itself made a needful turn towards the south, there was an equally needful
thing, a gully-hole with an iron trap to carry
off the rain that fell, or the spray that broke
upon the fabric ; and the outlet of this gully
was in the face of the masonry outside.
Carroway, not being gifted with a crooked
mind, had never dreamed that this little gut
might conduct the pulses of the air, like the
tyrant's ear, and that the trap at the end

might be a trap for him. Yet so it was; and by gently raising the movable iron frame at the top, a well-disposed person might hear every word that was spoken in the snug recess below. Cadman was well aware of this little fact, but left his commander to find it out.

The officer, always thinly clad, (both through the state of his wardrobe and his dread of effeminate comfort) settled his bony shoulders against the rough stonework, and his heels upon a groyne, and gave his subordinate a nod, which meant, "Make no fuss, but out with it." Cadman, a short square fellow with crafty eyes, began to do so.

"Captain, I have hit it off at last. Hackerbody put me wrong last time, through the wench he hath a hankering after. This time I got it, and no mistake, as right as if the villain lay asleep twixt you and me, and told us all about it with his tongue out; and a good thing for men of large families like me."

"All that I have heard such a number of times," his commander answered crustily, "that I whistle, as we used to do in a dead calm, Cadman. An old salt like you knows how little comes of that."

"There I don't quite agree with your Honour. I have known a hurricane come from whistling. But this time, there is no woman about it, and the penny have come down straight-forrard. New moon Tuesday next, and Monday we slips first into that snug little cave. He hath a' had his last good run."

"How much is coming this time, Cadman? I am sick and tired of those three caves. It is all old woman's talk of caves, while they are running south, upon the open beach."

"Captain, it is a big venture; the biggest of all the summer, I do believe. Two thousand pounds, if there is a penny, in it. The schooner, and the lugger, and the ketch, all to once, of purpose to send us scattering. But your Honour knows what we be after most. No woman in it this time, sir. The murder has been of the women, all along. When there is no woman I can see my way. We have got the right pig by the ear this time."

"John Cadman, your manner of speech is rude. You forget that your commanding officer has a wife and family, three-quarters of which are female. You will give me your information without any rude observations as to sex, of which you, as a married man, should be ashamed. A man and his wife are one flesh, Cadman; and therefore you are a woman yourself, and must labour not to disgrace yourself. Now don't look amazed, but consider these things. If you had not been in a flurry, like a woman, you would not have spoiled my dinner so. I will meet you at the outlook at six o'clock. I have business on hand of importance."

With these words Carroway hastened home, leaving Cadman to mutter his wrath, and then to growl it, when his officer was out of earshot.

" Never a day, nor an hour a'most without he insulteth of me. A woman indeed! Well, his wife may be a man, but what call hath he to speak of mine so ? John Cadman a woman, and one flesh with his wife! pretty news that would be for my missus!"

CHAPTER XIV.

SERIOUS CHARGES.

" STEPHEN, if it was anybody else—you would listen to me in a moment," said Mrs. Anerley to her lord, a few days after that little interview in the Bempton lane; " for instance, if it was poor Willie, how long would you be in believing it? But because it is Mary, you say 'pooh, pooh!' And I may as well talk to the old cracked churn."

" First time of all my born days," the farmer answered, with a pleasant smile, " that ever I was resembled to a churn. But a man's wife ought to know best about 'un."

" Stephen, it is not the churn—I mean you; and you never should attempt to ride off in that sort of way. I tell you Mary hath a mischief on her mind; and you never ought to bring up old churns to me. As long as I can carry almost anything in mind, I have been considered to be full of common sense. And what should I use it upon, Captain Anerley, without it was my own daughter?"

The farmer was always conquered when she called him " Captain Anerley." He took it to point at him as a pretender, a coxcomb fond of titles, a would-be officer, who took good care to hold aloof from fighting. And he knew in his heart that he loved to be called "Captain Anerley," by every one who meant it.

" My dear," he said, in a tone of submission, and with a look that grieved her; " the knowledge of such things is with you. I cannot enter into young maids' minds, any more than command a company."

" Stephen, you could do both, if you chose, better than ten of eleven who do it. For, Stephen, you have a very tender mind, and are not at all like a churn, my dear. That was my manner of speech, you ought to know; because from my youngest days I had a crowd of imagination. You remember that, Stephen, don't you?"

" I remember, Sophy, that in the old time

you never resembled me to a churn, let
alone a cracked one. You used to christen
me a pillar, and a tree, and a rock, and a
polished corner—but there, what's the odds,
when a man has done his duty? The names
of him makes no difference."

"'Twixt you and me, my dear," she said,
" nothing can make any difference. We know
one another too well for that. You are all
that I ever used to call you, before I knew
better about you; and when I used to
dwell upon your hair and your smile. You
know what I used to say of them now,
Stephen?"

"Most complimentary, highly complimentary! Another young woman brought me
word of it, and it made me stick firm, when
my mind was doubtful."

"And glad you ought to be that you did
stick firm. And you have the Lord to thank
for it, as well as your own sense. But no
time to talk of our old times now. They are
coming up again, with those younkers, I'm
afraid. Willie is like a Church; and Jack—
no chance of him getting the chance of it—
but Mary, your darling of the lot, our Mary
—her mind is unsettled, and a worry coming

over her; the same as with me, when I saw
you first."

"It is the Lord that directs those things,"
the farmer answered steadfastly; "and Mary
hath the sense of her mother, I believe. That
it is maketh me so fond on her. If the young
maid hath taken a fancy, it will pass, without a bit of substance to settle on. Why,
how many fancies had you, Sophy, before
you had the good luck to clap eyes on
me?"

"That is neither here nor there," his wife
replied audaciously; "how many times have
you asked such questions, which are no concern of yours? You could not expect me,
before ever I saw you, not to have any eyes
or ears. I had plenty to say for myself; and
I was not plain; and I acted accordingly."

Master Anerley thought about this, because
he had heard it, and thought of it, many times
before. He hated to think about anything
new, having never known any good come of
it; and his thoughts would rather flow than
fly, even in the fugitive brevity of youth.
And now, in his settled way, his practice was
to tread thought deeper into thought; as a
man in deep snow keeps the track of his own

boots; or as a child writes ink on pencil in
his earliest copy-books. "You acted according," he said; "and Mary might act
according to you, mother."

"How can you talk so, Stephen? That
would be a different thing altogether. Young
girls are not a bit like what they used to be
in my time. No steadiness, no diligence, no
duty to their parents. Gadding about is all
they think of, and light-headed chatter, and
saucy ribbons."

"May be so with some of them. But I
never see none of that in Mary."

"Mary is a good girl, and well brought
up," her mother could not help admitting;
"and fond of her home, and industrious. But
for all that, she must be looked after sharply.
And who can look after a child like her
mother? I can tell you one thing, Master
Stephen, your daughter Mary has more will
of her own than the rest of your family all
put together, including even your own good
wife."

"Prodigious!" cried the farmer, while he
rubbed his hands and laughed, "prodigious;
and a man might say impossible. A young
lass like Mary, such a coaxing little poppet,

as tender as a lambkin, and as soft as wool!"

"Flannel won't only run one way; no more won't Mary," said her mother; "I know her better a long sight than you do; and I say if ever Mary sets her heart on any one, have him she will, be he cow-boy, thief, or chimney-sweep. So now you know what to expect, Master Anerley."

Stephen Anerley never made light of his wife's opinions in those few cases wherein they differed from his own. She agreed with him so generally, that in common fairness he thought very highly of her wisdom; and the present subject was one upon which she had an especial right to be heard.

"Sophy," he said, as he set up his coat to be off to a cutting of clover on the hill—for no reaping would begin yet for another month—"the things you have said shall abide in my mind. Only you be a-watching of the little wench. Harry Tanfield is the man I would choose for her of all others. But I never would force any husband on a lass; though stern would I be to force a bad one off, or one in an unfit walk of life. No inkle in your mind who it is, or would'st have told me ? "

" Well, I may, or I may not. I never like to speak promiscuous. You have the first right to know what I think. But I beg you to let me be awhile. Not even to you, Steve, would I say it, without more to go upon than there is yet. I might do the lass a great wrong in my surmising; and then you would visit my mistake on me ; for she is the apple of your eye, no doubt."

" There is never such another maid in all York county; nor in England, to my thinking."

" She is my daughter as well as yours, and I would be the last to make cheap of her. I will not say another word until I know. But if I am right—which the Lord forbid— we shall both be ashamed of her, Stephen."

" The Lord forbid! The Lord forbid ! Amen. I will not hear another word." The farmer snatched up his hat, and made off with a haste unusual for him, while his wife sate down, and crossed her arms, and began to think rather bitterly. For, without any dream of such a possibility, she was jealous sometimes of her own child. Presently the

farmer rushed back again, triumphant with a
new idea. His eyes were sparkling, and his
step full of spring, and a brisk smile shone
upon his strong and ruddy face.

·"What a pair of stupes we must be to go
on so!" he cried, with a couple of bright
guineas in his hand; "Mary hath not had a
new frock even, going on now for a year and
a half. Sophy, it is enough to turn a maid
into thinking of any sort of mischief. Take
you these, and make everything right. I was
saving them up for her birthday, but maybe
another will turn up by that. My dear, you
take them, and never be afeared."

"Stephen, you may leave them, if you like.
I shall not be in any haste to let them go.
Either give them to the lass yourself, or leave
it to me purely. She shall not have a six-
pence, unless it is deserved."

"Of course, I leave it in your hands, wife.
I never come between you and your children.
But young folk go piping always after money
now; and even our Mary might be turning
sad without it."

He hastened off again, without hearing any
more; for he knew that some hours of strong
labour were before him; and to meet them

with a heavy heart would be almost a new
thing for him.   Some time ago he had begun
to hold the plough of heaviness, through the
difficult looseness of Willie's staple, and the
sudden maritime slope of Jack ; yet he held
on steadily through all this, with the strength
of homely courage.   But if in the pride of
his heart, his Mary, he should find no better
than a crooked furrow, then truly the labour
of his latter days would be the dull round of
a mill-horse.

Now Mary, in total ignorance of that
council held concerning her, and even of her
mother's bad suspicions, chanced to come in
at the front porch-door, soon after her father
set off to his meadows by way of the back-
yard. Having been hard at work among her
flowers, she was come to get a cupful of milk
for herself, and the cheery content and general good-will encouraged by the gardener's
gentle craft, were smiling on her rosy lips
and sparkling in her eyes. Her dress was as
plain as plain could be, a lavender twill cut
and fitted by herself, and there was not an
ornament about her that came from any
other hand than nature's. But simple grace
of movement, and light elegance of figure, fair

curves of gentle face, and loving kindness of expression, gladdened with the hope of youth —what did these want with smart dresses, golden brooches, and two guineas? Her mother almost thought of this, when she called Mary into the little parlour. And the two guineas lay upon the table.

"Mary, can you spare a little time to talk with me? You seem wonderfully busy, as usual."

"Mother, will you never make allowance for my flowers? They depend upon the weather, and they must have things accordingly."

"Very well, let them think about what they want next, while you sit down awhile, and talk with me."

The girl was vexed; for to listen to a lecture already manifest in her mother's eyes, was a far less agreeable job than gardening. And the lecture would have done as well by candle-light, which seldom can be said of any gardening. However, she took off her hat, and sat down, without the least sign of impatience, and without any token of guilt, as her mother saw, and yet stupidly proceeded just the same.

"Mary," she began, with a gaze of stern
discretion, which the girl met steadfastly and
pleasantly; "you know that I am your own
mother, and bound to look after you well,
while you are so very young. For though
you are sensible some ways, Mary, in years
and in experience what are you but a child?
Of the traps of the world, and the wickedness
of people, you can have no knowledge. You
always think the best of everybody; which is
a very proper thing to do, and what I have
always brought you up to, and never would
dream of discouraging. And with such
examples as your father and your mother,
you must be perverse to do otherwise. Still
it is my duty to warn you, Mary, and you are
getting old enough to want it, that the world
is not made up of fathers, and mothers,
brothers, and sisters, and good uncles. There
are always bad folk who go prowling about
like wolves in—wolves in—what is it—"

"Sheep's clothing"—the maiden sug-
gested with a smile, and then dropped her
eyes maliciously.

"How dare you be pert, miss, correcting
your own mother? Do I ever catch you
reading of your Bible? But you seem to

know so much about it, perhaps you have
met some of them?"

"How can I tell, mother, when you won't
tell me?"

"I tell you indeed! It is your place to
tell me, I think. And what is more, I insist
at once upon knowing all about it. What
makes you go on in the way that you are
doing? Do you take me for a drumledore, you
foolish child? On Tuesday afternoon I saw
you sewing with a double-thread. Your father
had potato-eyes upon his plate on Sunday; and
which way did I see you trying to hang up a
dish-cover? But that is nothing; fifty things
you go wandering about in; and always out,
on some pretence, as if the roof you were born
under was not big enough for you. And
then your eyes—I have seen your eyes flash
up, as if you were fighting; and the bosom of
your Sunday frock was loose in church two
buttons; it was not hot at all to speak of,
and there was a wasp next pew. All these
things make me unhappy, Mary. My darling,
tell me what it is."

Mary listened with great amazement to
this catalogue of crimes. At the time of
their commission, she had never even thought

of them; although she was vexed with herself, when she saw one eye—for in verity
that was all—of a potato upon her father's
plate. Now she blushed, when she heard of
the buttons of her frock—which was only
done because of tightness, and showed how
long she must have worn it—but as to the
double-thread, she was sure that nothing of
that sort could have happened.

"Why, mother dear," she said, quite
softly, coming up in her coaxing way, which
nobody could resist, because it was true and
gentle lovingness; "you know a hundred
times more than I do. I have never known
of any of the sad mistakes, you speak of;
except about the potato-eye, and then I had
a round-pointed knife. But I want to make
no excuses, mother; and there is nothing the
matter with me. Tell me what you mean
about the wolves."

"My child," said her mother, whose face
she was kissing, while they both went on
with talking; "it is no good trying to get
over me. Either you have something on
your mind, or you have not—which is it?"

"Mother, what can I have on my mind?
I have never hurt any one, and never mean to

do it. Every one is kind to me, and everybody likes me; and of course I like them all again. And I always have plenty to do, in and out, as you take very good care, dear mother. My father loves me; and so do you, a great deal more than I deserve perhaps; I am happy in a Sunday frock that wants more stuff to button; and I have only one trouble in all the world. When I think of the other girls I see "—

"Never mind them, my dear. What is your one trouble?"

"Mother, as if you could help knowing! About my dear brother Jack, of course. Jack was so wonderfully good to me! I would walk on my hands and knees all the way to York, to get a single glimpse of him."

"You would never get as far as the rickyard hedge. You children talk such nonsense. Jack ran away of his own free will, and out of downright contrariness. He has repented of it only once, I dare say; and that has been ever since he did it, and every time he thought of it. I wish he was home again with all my heart, for I cannot bear to lose my children. And Jack was as good a boy as need be, when he got everything his own way. Mary, is that your only trouble? Stand where I can see you plainly, and tell me every word the truth. Put your hair back from your eyes now, like the catechism."

"If I were saying fifty catechisms, what more could I do than speak the truth?" Mary asked this with some little vexation; while she stood up proudly before her mother, and clasped her hands behind her back. "I have told you everything I know, except one little thing, which I am not sure about."

"What little thing, if you please? And how can you help being sure about it, positive as you are about everything?"

"Mother, I mean that I have not been sure whether I ought to tell you; and I meant to tell my father first, when there could be no mischief."

"Mary, I can scarcely believe my ears. To tell your father, before your mother; and not even him, until nothing could be done to stop it, which you call 'mischief'! I insist upon knowing at once what it is. I have felt that you were hiding something. How very unlike you, how unlike a child of mine!"

"You need not disturb yourself, mother

dear. It is nothing of any importance to me,
though to other people it might be. And
that is the reason why I kept it to myself."

"Oh, we shall come to something by-and-
by! One would really think you were older
than your mother. Now, miss, if you please,
let us judge of your discretion. What is it
that you have been hiding so long?"

Mary's face grew crimson now, but with
anger rather than with shame; she had never
thought twice about Robin Lyth, with anything warmer than pity; but this was the
very way to drive her into dwelling in a mis-
chievous manner upon him.

"What I have been hiding," she said
most distinctly, and steadfastly looking at her
mother, "is only that I have had two talks
with the great free-trader, Robin Lyth."

"That arrant smuggler! That leader of
all outlaws! You have been meeting him on
the sly!"

"Certainly not. But I met him once by
chance; and then, as a matter of business,
I was forced to meet him again, dear
mother."

"These things are too much for me," Mrs.
Anerley said decisively; "when matters have

come to such a pass, I must beg your dear
father to see to them."

"Very well, mother; I would rather have
it so.   May I go now and make an end of my
gardening?"

"Certainly; as soon as you have made
an end of me; as you must quite have laid
your plans to do.   I have seen too much
to be astonished any more.   But to think
that a child of mine, my one and only
daughter, who looks as if butter wouldn't
melt in her mouth, should be hand in glove
with the wickedest smuggler of the age, the
rogue everybody shoots at, but cannot hit
him, because he was born to be hanged—the
by-name, the by-word, the by-blow, Robin
Lyth!"   Mrs. Anerley covered her face with
both hands.

"How would you like your own second
cousin," said Mary, plucking up her spirit,
"your own second cousin, Mistress Cockscroft,
to hear you speak so of the man that supports
them, at the risk of his life, every hour of it?
He may be doing wrong; it is not for me to
say, but he does it very well, and he does it
nobly.   And what did you show me in your
drawer, dear mother?   And what did you

wear, when that very cruel man, Captain Carroway, came here to dine on Sunday ? "

" You wicked, undutiful child ! Go away. I wish to have nothing more to say to you."

" No, I will not go away," cried Mary, with her resolute spirit in her eyes and brow; " when false and cruel charges are brought against me, I have the right to speak, and I will use it. I am not hand in glove with Robin Lyth, or any other Robin. I think a little more of myself than that. If I have done any wrong, I will meet it, and be sorry, and submit to any punishment. I ought to have told you before perhaps; that is the worst you can say of it. But I never attached much importance to it; and when a man is hunted so, was I to join his enemies ? I have only seen him twice ; the first time by purest accident; and the second time to give him back a piece of his own property. And I took my brother with me; but he ran away, as usual."

" Of course, of course. Every one to blame but you, miss. However, we shall see what your father has to say. You have very nearly taken all my breath away; but I shall expect the whole sky to tumble in upon us, if Captain Anerley approves of Robin Lyth as a sweetheart for his daughter."

" I never thought of Captain Lyth; and Captain Lyth never thought of me. But I can tell you one thing, mother—if you wanted to make me think of him, you could not do it better than by speaking so unjustly."

" After that perhaps you will go back to your flowers. I have heard that they grow very fine ones in Holland. Perhaps you have got some smuggled tulips, my dear."

Mary did not condescend to answer, but said to herself as she went to work again,— " Tulips in August! That is like the rest of it. However, I am not going to be put out, when I feel that I have not done a single bit of harm." And she tried to be happy with her flowers; but could not enter into them, as before.

Mistress Anerley was as good as her word, at the very first opportunity. Her husband returned from the clover-stack, tired and hungry, and angry with a man, who had taken too much beer, and ran at him with a pitchfork; angry also with his own son Willie, for not being anywhere in the way to help. He did not complain; and his wife knew at once that

he ought to have done so, to obtain relief.
She perceived that her own discourse about
their daughter was still on his mind, and
would require working off, before any more
was said about it. And she felt as sure as if
she saw it, that in his severity against poor
Willie—for not doing things that were beneath him—her master would take Mary's
folly as a joke, and fall upon her brother, who
was so much older, for not going on to protect and guide her. So she kept till after
supper-time her mouthful of bad tidings.

And when the farmer heard it all, as he did
before going to sleep that night, he had
smoked three pipes of tobacco, and was calm,
he had sipped (for once in a way) a little
Hollands, and was hopeful. And though he
said nothing about it, he felt, that without any
order of his, or so much as the faintest desire
to be told of it, neither of these petty comforts would bear to be rudely examined of its
duty. He hoped for the best, and he believed
the best; and if the king was cheated, why, his
loyal subject was the same, and the women
were their masters.

"Have no fear, no fear," he muttered back
through the closing gate of sleep; "Mary

knows her business—business—" and he
buzzed it off into a snore.

In the morning, however, he took a stronger
and more serious view of the case, pronouncing
that Mary was only a young lass, and no one
could ever tell about young lasses. And he
quite fell into his wife's suggestion, that the
maid could be spared till harvest-time, of
which (even with the best of weather) there
was little chance now for another six weeks,
the season being late and backward. So it
was resolved between them both, that the
girl should go on the following day for a visit
to her Uncle Popplewell, some miles the other
side of Filey. No invitation was required :
for Mr. and Mrs. Popplewell, a snug and comfortable pair, were only too glad to have their
niece, and had often wanted to have her altogether; but the farmer would never hear of
that.

CHAPTER XV.

CAUGHT AT LAST.

WHILE these little things were doing thus, the
coast from the mouth of the Tees to that of
the Humber, and even the inland parts, were
in a great stir of talk and work, about events
impending. It must not be thought that
Flamborough, although it was Robin's dwell-
ing-place—so far as he had any—was the
principal scene of his operations, or the stronghold of his enterprise. On the contrary, his
liking was for quiet coves near Scarborough,
or even to the north of Whitby, when the
wind and tide were suitable. And for this
there were many reasons, which are not of any
moment now.

One of them showed fine feeling, and much
delicacy on his part. He knew that Flamborough was a place of extraordinary honesty,

where every one of his buttons had been safe, and would have been so for ever; and strictly as he believed in the virtue of his own free importation, it was impossible for him not to learn that certain people thought otherwise, or acted as if they did so. From the troubles which such doubts might cause he strove to keep the natives free.

Flamburians scarcely understood this large-ness of good-will to them. Their instincts told them that free-trade was every Briton's privilege; and they had the finest set of donkeys on the coast for landing it. But none the more did any of them care to make a movement towards it. They were satisfied with their own old way—to cast the net their father cast, and bait the hook as it was baited on their good grandfather's thumb.

Yet even Flamborough knew that now a mighty enterprise was in hand. It was said, without any contradiction, that young Captain Robin had laid a wager of one hundred guineas with the worshipful mayor of Scarborough, and the commandant of the castle, that before the new moon he would land on Yorkshire coast, without firing pistol or drawing steel, free goods to the value of two

thousand pounds, and carry them inland
safely. And Flamborough believed that he
would do it.

Dr. Upround's house stood well, as rectories
generally contrive to do. No place in Flamborough parish could hope to swindle the
wind of its vested right, or to embezzle much
treasure of the sun; but the parsonage made
a good effort to do both, and sometimes for
three days together got the credit of succeed-
ing. And the dwellers therein, who felt the
edge of the difference outside their own walls,
not only said, but thoroughly believed, that
they lived in a little Goshen.

For the house was well settled in a wrinkle
of the hill expanding southward, and en-
couraging the noon. From the windows a
pleasant glimpse might be obtained of the
broad and tranquil anchorage, peopled with
white or black, according as the sails went up
or down; for the rectory stood to the southward of the point, as the rest of Flamborough surely must have stood, if built by
any other race than armadilloes. But to
see all those vessels and be sure what
they were doing, the proper place was a
little snug "gazebo," chosen and made by the

Doctor himself, near the crest of the gulley he inhabited.

Here upon a genial summer day—when it came, as it sometimes dared to do—was the finest little nook upon the Yorkshire coast for watching what Virgil calls " the sail-winged sea." Not that a man could see round the Head, unless his own were gifted with very crooked eyes; but without doing that (which would only have disturbed the tranquillity of his prospect) there was plenty to engage him in the peaceful spread of comparatively wave-less waters. Here might he see long vessels rolling, not with great misery, but just enough to make him feel happy in the firmness of his bench, and little jolly-boats it was more jolly to be out of, and far-away heads giving genial bobs, and sea-legs straddled in predica-ments desirable rather for study than for practice. All was highly picturesque and nice, and charming for the critic who had never got to do it.

"Now, papa, you must come this very moment," cried Miss Janetta Upround (the daughter of the house, and indeed the only daughter), with a gush of excitement, rushing into the study of this deeply-read divine;

" there is something doing that I cannot understand. You must bring up the spy-glass at once, and explain. I am sure that there is something very wrong."

"In the parish, my dear?" the rector asked, with a feeble attempt at malice, for he did not want to be disturbed just now, and for weeks he had tried (with very poor success) to make Janetta useful; for she had no gift in that way.

"No, not in the parish at all, papa; unless it runs out under water, as I am certain it ought to do, and make every one of those ships pay tithe. If the law was worth anything, they would have to do it. They get all the good out of our situation, and they save whole thousands of pounds at a time, and they never pay a penny, nor even hoist a flag, unless the day is fine, and the flag wants drying. But come along, papa, now. I really cannot wait; and they will have done it all without us."

"Janetta, take the glass and get the focus. I will come presently, presently. In about two minutes, by the time that you are ready."

"Very well, papa. It is very good of you. I see quite clearly what you want to do; and

I hope you will do it.   But you promise not
to play another game now?"

"My dear, I will promise that with pleasure.   Only do please be off about your
business."

The rector was a most inveterate and
insatiable chess-player.   In the household,
rather than by it, he was, as a matter of lofty
belief, supposed to be deeply engaged with
theology, or magisterial questions of almost
equal depth, or (to put it at the lowest) paro-
chial affairs, the while he was solidly and
seriously engaged in getting up the sound
defence to some continental gambit.   And
this, not only to satisfy himself upon some
point of theory, but from a nearer and dearer
point of view—for he never did like to be
beaten.

At present he was labouring to discover
the proper defence to a new and slashing
form of the Algaier gambit, by means of
which Robin Lyth had won every game in
which he had the move, upon their last encounter.   The great free-trader, while a boy,
had shown an especial aptitude for chess; and
even as a child he had seemed to know the
men, when first, by some accident, he saw

them. The rector being struck by this exception to the ways of childhood—whose manner it is to take chessmen for " dollies," or roll them about like nine-pins—at once included in the education of " Izunsabe," which he took upon himself, a course of elemental doctrine in the one true game. And the boy fought his way up at such a pace, that he jumped from odds of queen and rook, to pawn and two moves, in less than two years. And now he could almost give odds to his tutor, though he never presumed to offer them ; and trading as he did with enlightened merchants of large continental sea-ports, who had plenty of time on their hands and played well, he imported new openings of a dash and freedom which swallowed the ground up under the feet of the steady-going players, who had never seen a book upon their favourite subject. Of course it was competent to all these to decline such fiery onslaught ; but chivalry and the true love of analysis (which without may none play chess) compelled the acceptance of the challenge, even with a trembling forecast of the taste of dust.

" Never mind," said Dr. Upround, as he

rose and stretched himself, a good straight man of three-score years, with silver hair that shone like silk; "it has not come to me yet; but it must, with a little more perseverance. At Cambridge I beat everybody; and who is this uncircumcised—at least, I beg his pardon, for I did myself baptize him—but who is Robin Lyth, to mate his pastor and his master? All these gambits are like a night attack. If once met properly and expelled, you are in the very heart of the enemy's camp. He has left his own watch-fires to rush at yours. The next game I play, I shall be sure to beat him."

Fully convinced of this great truth, he took a strong oak-staff, and hastened to obey his daughter. Miss Janetta Upround had not only learned by nature, but also had been carefully taught by her parents, and by every one, how to get her own way always, and to be thanked for taking it. But she had such a happy nature, full of kindness, and good will, that other people's wishes always seemed to flow into her own, instead of being swept aside. Over her father her government was in no sort constitutional, nor even a quiet despotism sweetened with liberal

illusions, but as pure a piece of autocracy as
the Continent could itself contain, in the time
of this first Napoleon.

"Papa, what a time you have been, to be
sure!" she exclaimed, as the Doctor came
gradually up, probing his way in perfect
leisure, and fragrant still of that gambit;
" one would think that your parish was on
dry land altogether, while the better half of
it, as they call themselves—though the
women are in righteousness, the better half a
hundred-fold—"

"My dear, do try to talk with some little
sense of arithmetic, if no other. A hundred-
fold the half would be the unit multiplied by
fifty. Not to' mention that there can be no
better half—"

"Yes, there can, papa, ever so many; and
you may see one in mamma every day. Now
you put one eye to this glass; and the half is
better than the whole. With both, you see
nothing; with one, you see better, fifty times
better than with both before. Don't talk
of arithmetic after that. It is Algebra now,
and quod demonstrandum."

"To reason with the less worthy gender is
degeneration of reason. What would they

have said in the Senate-house, Janetta?
However, I will obey your orders. What
am I to look at?"

"A tall and very extraordinary man, striking his arms out, thus and thus. I never saw
any one looking so excited; and he flourishes
a long sword now and again, as if he would
like to cut everybody's head off. There he has
been going from ship to ship, for an hour or
more, with a long white boat, and a lot of men
jumping after him. Every one seems to be
scared of him, and he stumps along the
deck, just as if he were on springs, and one
spring longer than the other. You see that
heavy brig outside the rest, painted with ten
port-holes; well, she began to make sail, and
run away, but he fired a gun—quite a real can-
non; and she had to come back again, and
drop her colours. Oh, is it some very great
admiral, papa? Perhaps Lord Nelson himself; I would go and be sea-sick for three
days, to see Lord Nelson. Papa, it must be
Lord Nelson."

"My dear, Lord Nelson is a little, short
man, with a very brisk walk, and one arm
gone. Now let me see who this can be.
Whereabout is he now, Janetta?"

" Do you see that clumsy-looking schooner, papa, just behind a pilot-boat? He is just in front of her foremast—making such a fuss—"

"What eyes you have got, my child! You see better without the glass than I do with it.—Oh now I have him! Why, I might have guessed. Of course it is that very active man and vigilant officer, Lieutenant Carroway."

"Captain Carroway from Bridlington, papa! Why, what can he be doing with such authority? I have often heard of him, but I thought he was only a Coast-guard."

"He is, as you say, showing great authority, and I fear using very bad language, for which he is quite celebrated. However, the telescope refuses to repeat it, for which it is much to be commended. But every allowance must be made for a man who has to deal with a wholly uncultivated race, and not of natural piety, like ours."

"Well, papa, I doubt if ours have too much, though you always make such lambs of them. But let me look again, please; and do tell me what he can be doing there."

"You know that the Revenue-Officers

must take the law into their own hands
sometimes.   There have lately been certain
rumours of some contraband proceedings on
the Yorkshire coast; not in Flamborough
parish, of course, and perhaps, probably I
may say, a long way off—"

"Papa dear, will you never confess that
free-trade prevails, and flourishes greatly,
even under your own dear nose?"

"Facts do not warrant me in any such
assertion.   If the fact were so, it must have
been brought officially before me.   I decline
to listen to uncharitable rumours.   But
however that matter may be, there are
officers on the spot to deal with it.   My
commission, as a Justice of the Peace,
gives me no cognizance of offences—if such
there are—upon the high seas.   Ah, you see
something particular; my dear, what is
it?"

"Captain Carroway has found something,
or somebody, of great importance.   He has
got a man by the collar, and he is absolutely
dancing with delight.   Ah, there he goes,
dragging him along the deck, as if he were a
cod-fish, or a conger.   And now, I declare, he
is lashing his arms and legs, with a great

thick rope. Papa, is that legal, without even a warrant?"

"I can hardly say how far his powers may extend; and he is just the man to extend them farther. I only hope not to be involved in the matter. Maritime law is not my province."

"But, papa, it is much within three miles of the shore; if that has got anything to do with it. My goodness me! They are all coming here, I am almost sure that they will apply to you. Yes, two boat-loads of people racing to get their oars out, and to be here first. Where are your spectacles, dear papa? You had better go and get up the law, before they come. You will scarcely have time, they are coming so fast—a white boat, and a black boat. The prisoner is in the white boat, and the officer has got him by the collar still. The men in the white boat will want to commit him; and the men in the black boat are his friends, no doubt, coming for a habeas-corpus—"

"My dear, what nonsense you do talk; what has a simple Justice of the Peace—"

"Never mind that, papa, my facts are sound; sounder than yours about smuggling,

I fear. But do hurry in, and get up the law. I will go and lock both gates, to give you more time."

"Do nothing of the kind, Janetta. A magistrate should be accessible always; and how can I get up the law, without knowing what it is to be about—or even a clerk to help me? And perhaps they are not coming here at all. They may be only landing their prisoner."

"If that were it, they would not be coming so; but rowing towards the proper place—Bridlington Quay, where their station-house is. Papa, you are in for it, and I am getting eager. May I come and hear all about it? I should be a great support to you, you know. And they would tell the truth so much better."

"Janetta, what are you dreaming of? It may even be a case of secrecy."

"Secrecy, papa, with two boat-loads of men, and about thirty ships involved in it! Oh, do let me hear all about it!"

"Whatever it may be, your presence is not required, and would be improper. Unless I should happen to want a book; and in that case I might ring for you."

"Oh, do, papa, do! No one else can ever find them. Promise me now, that you will want a book. If I am not there, there will be no justice done. I wish you severely to reprimand, whatever the facts of the case may be, and even to punish, if you can, that tall, lame, violent, ferocious man, for dragging the poor fellow about like that, and cutting him with ropes, when completely needless, and when he was quite at his mercy. It is my opinion that the other man does not deserve one bit of it; and whatever the law may be, papa, your duty is to strain it benevolently, and question every syllable upon the stronger side."

"Perhaps I had better resign, my dear, upon condition that you shall be appointed in the stead of me. It might be a popular measure, and would secure universal justice."

"Papa, I would do justice to myself—which is a thing you never do. But here, they are landing; and they hoist him out, as if he were a sack, or a thing without a joint. They could scarcely be harder with a man compelled to be hanged to-morrow morning."

"Condemned is what you mean, Janetta. You never will understand the use of words. What a nice magistrate you would make!"

"There can be no more correct expression. Would any man be hanged, if he were not compelled? Papa, you say the most illegal things sometimes. Now, please to go in, and get up your legal points. Let me go and meet those people, for you. I will keep them waiting, till you are quite ready."

"My dear, you will go to your room, and try to learn a little patience. You begin to be too pat with your own opinions; which in a young lady is ungraceful. There, you need not cry, my darling, because your opinions are always sensible, and I value them very highly; but still you must bear in mind that you are but a girl."

"And behave accordingly, as they say. Nobody can do more so. But though I am only a girl, papa, can you put your hand upon a better one?"

"Certainly not, my dear; for going down hill, I can always depend on you."

Suiting the action to the word, Dr. Upround, whose feet were a little touched with gout, came down from his outlook to his kitchen-garden, and thence through the shrubbery, back to his own study; where, with a little sigh, he put away his chessmen, and heartily hoped that it might not be his favourite adversary who was coming before him, to be sent to jail. For although the good rector had a warm regard, and even affection, for Robin Lyth, as a waif cast into his care, and then a pupil wonderfully apt (which breeds love in the teacher), and after that a most gallant and highly distinguished young parishioner; with all this it was a difficulty for him to be ignorant that the law was hostile. More than once he had striven hard to lead the youth into some better path of life, and had even induced him to "follow the sea" for a short time, in the merchant-service. But the force of nature, and of circumstances, had very soon prevailed again, and Robin returned to his old pursuits, with larger experience, and seamanship improved.

A violent ringing at the gate-bell, followed by equal urgency upon the front-door, apprised the kind magistrate of a sharp call on his faculties, and perhaps a most unpleasant one. "The poor boy," he said to himself; "poor boy! From Carroway's excitement I greatly fear that it is indeed poor Robin. How many a grand game have we had! His new variety of that fine gambit scarcely beginning to be analyzed; and if I commit him to the meeting next week, when shall we ever meet again? It will seem as if I did it, because he won three games; and I certainly was a little vexed with him. However, I must be stern, stern, stern. Show them in, Betsy; I am quite prepared."

A noise, and a sound of strong language in the hall, and a dragging of something on the oilcloth, led up to the entry of a dozen rough men, pushed on by at least another dozen.

"You will have the manners to take off your hats," said the magistrate, with all his dignity; "not from any undue deference to me, but common respect to his Majesty."

"Off with your covers, you sons of "—something, shouted a loud voice; and then the lieutenant, with his blade still drawn, stood before them.

"Sheathe your sword, sir," said Dr. Up-round, in a voice which amazed the officer.

"I beg your Worship's pardon," he began,

with his grim face flushing purple, but his
sword laid where it should have been; "but
if you knew half of the worry I have had,
you would not care to rebuke me. Cadman,
have you got him by the neck? Keep your
knuckles into him, while I make my deposition."

"Cast that man free. I receive no deposi-
tions, with a man half-strangled before me."

The men of the coast-guard glanced at
their commander, and, receiving a surly
nod, obeyed. But the prisoner could not
stand as yet; he gasped for breath, and some
one set him on a chair.

"Your Worship, this is a mere matter of
form," said Carroway, still keeping eyes on
his prey; "if I had my own way, I would not
trouble you at all, and I believe it to be quite
needless. For this man is an outlaw felon,
and not entitled to any grace of law; but I
must obey my orders."

"Certainly you must, Lieutenant Carroway; even though you are better acquainted
with the law. You are ready to be sworn.
Take this book, and follow me."

This being done, the worthy magistrate
prepared to write down what the gallant

officer might say; which, in brief, came to this, that having orders to seize Robin Lyth, wherever he might find him, and having sure knowledge that said Robin was on board of a certain schooner vessel, the "Elizabeth," of Goole, the which he had laden with goods liable to duty, he, Charles Carroway, had gently laid hands on him, and brought him to the nearest Justice of the Peace, to obtain an order of commitment.

All this, at fifty times the length here given, Lieutenant Carroway deposed on oath, while his Worship, for want of a clerk, set it down in his own very neat handwriting. But several very coaly-looking men, who could scarcely be taught to keep silence, observed that the magistrate smiled once or twice; and this made them wait a bit, and wink at one another.

"Very clear indeed, Lieutenant Carroway," said Dr. Upround, with spectacles on nose; "good sir, have the kindness to sign your deposition. It may become my duty to commit the prisoner, upon identification. Of that I must have evidence, confirmatory evidence. But first we will hear what he has to say. Robin Lyth, stand forward."

" Me no Robin Lyth, sar; no Robin man
or woman," cried the captive, trying very
hard to stand; " me only a poor Français,
make liberty to what you call—row, row,
sweem, sweem, sail, sail, from la belle France;
for why, for why, there is no import to
nobody."

" Your Worship, he is always going on
about imports," Cadman said [respectfully;
" that is enough to show who he is."

" You may trust me to know him," cried
Lieutenant Carroway; " my fine fellow, no
more of that stuff! He can pass himself off
for any countryman whatever. He knows
all their jabber, sir, better than his own. Put
a cork between his teeth, Hackerbody. I
never did see such a noisy rogue. He is
Robin Lyth all over."

" I'll be blest if he is; nor under nay-
ther," cried the biggest of the coaly men;
" this here froggy come out of a Chaise and
Mary, as had run up from Dunkirk. I know
Robin Lyth as well as our own figure-head.
But what good to try reason with that there
revenue hofficer?"

At this, all his friends set a good laugh up,
and wanted to give him a cheer for such a

speech ; but, that being hushed, they were satisfied with condemning his organs of sight, and their own, quite fairly.

"Lieutenant Carroway," his Worship said, amidst an impressive silence; " I greatly fear that you have allowed zeal, my dear sir, to outrun discretion. Robin Lyth is a young, and in many ways highly respected, parishioner of mine. He may have been guilty of casual breaches of the laws concerning importation, laws which fluctuate from year to year, and require deep knowledge of legislation, both to observe, and to administer. I heartily trust that you may not suffer from having discharged your duty, in a manner most truly exemplary, if only the example had been the right one. This gentleman is no more Robin Lyth, than I am."

CHAPTER XVI.

DISCIPLINE ASSERTED.

As soon as his troublesome visitors were gone, the rector sat down in his deep-arm chair, laid aside his spectacles, and began to think. His face, while he thought, lost more and more of the calm and cheerful expression, which made it so pleasant a face to gaze upon ; and he sighed, without knowing it, at some dark ideas, and gave a little shake of his grand old head. The revenue-officer had called his favourite pupil and cleverest parishioner " a felon outlaw ;" and if that were so, Robin Lyth was no less than a convicted criminal, and must not be admitted within his doors. Formerly the regular penalty for illicit importation had been the forfeiture of the goods, when caught ; and the smugglers (unless they made resistance, or carried fire-arms) were allowed

to escape, and retrieve their bad luck, which
they very soon contrived to do. And as yet,
upon this part of the coast, they had not
been guilty of atrocious crimes, such as the
smugglers of Sussex and Hampshire, who
must have been utter fiends, committed,
thereby raising all the land against them.
Dr. Upround had heard of no proclamation,
exaction, or even capias, issued against this
young free-trader; and he knew well enough
that the worst offenders were not the bold
seamen who contracted for the run, nor the
people of the coast who were hired for the
carriage, but the rich indwellers who provided
all the money, and received the lion's share
of all the profits. And with these the law
never even tried to deal. However, the magistrate parson resolved, that, in spite of all the
interest of tutorship and chess-play, and even
all the influence of his wife and daughter,
(who were hearty admirers of brave smuggling), he must either reform this young man,
or compel him to keep at a distance, which
would be very sad.

Meanwhile the lieutenant had departed in
a fury, which seemed to be incapable of growing any worse. Never an oath did he utter

all the way to the landing, where his boat was left; and his men, who knew how much that meant, were afraid to do more than just wink at one another. Even the sailors of the collier schooner forbore to jeer him, until he was afloat, when they gave him three fine rounds of mock-cheers, to which the poor Frenchman contributed a shriek. For this man had been most inhospitably treated, through his strange but undeniable likeness to a perfidious Briton.

"Home!" cried the officer, glowering at those fellows, while his men held their oars, and were ready to rush at them. "Home with a will! Give way, men!" And not another word he spoke, till they touched the steps at Bridlington. Then he fixed stern eyes upon Cadman, who vainly strove to meet them, and he said, "Come to me, in one hour and a half." Cadman touched his hat without an answer, saw to the boat, and then went home along the quay.

Carroway, though of a violent temper, especially when laughed at, was not of that steadfast and sedentary wrath, which chews the cud of grievances, and feeds upon it in a shady place. He had a good wife—though a little over-clean—and seven fine-appetited children, who gave him the greatest pleasure in providing victuals. Also, he had his pipe, and his quiet corners, sacred to the atmosphere, and the private thoughts of Carroway. And here he would often be ambitious even now, perceiving no good reason why he might not yet command a line-of-battle ship, and run up his own flag, and nobly tread his own lofty quarter-deck. If so, he would have Mrs. Carroway on board, and not only on the boards, but at them; so that a challenge should be issued every day, for any other ship in all the service, to display white so wholly spotless, and black so void of streakiness. And while he was dwelling upon personal matters—which after all concerned the nation most—he had tried very hard to discover any reason (putting paltry luck aside) why Horatio Nelson should be a Lord, and what was more to the purpose, an admiral, while Charles Carroway (his old shipmate, and in every way superior, who could eat him at a mouthful, if only he were good enough) should now be no more than a 'long-shore lieutenant, and a Jonathan Wild of the Revenue. However, as for envying Nelson, the Lord knew that he would not give his little Geraldine's worst frock, for all the fellow's grand coat-of-arms, and freedom in a snuff-box, and golden shields, and devices, this, that, and the other, with Pharaoh of Egypt to support them.

To this conclusion he was fairly come, after a good meal, and with the second glass of the finest Jamaica pine-apple rum—which he drank from pure principle, because it was not smuggled—steaming and scenting the blue curls of his pipe, when his admirable wife came in to say that on no account would she interrupt him.

" My dear, I am busy, and am very glad to hear it. Pish ! where have I put all those accounts ? "

" Charles, you are not doing any accounts. When you have done your pipe and glass, I wish to say a quiet word or two. I am sure that there is not a woman in a thousand—"

"Matilda, I know it. Nor one in fifty thousand. You are very good at figures ; will you take this sheet away with you ? Eight o'clock will be quite time enough for it."

" My dear, I am always too pleased to do whatever I can to help you. But I must

talk to you now; really I must say a few
words about something, tired as you may be,
Charles, and well deserving of a little good
sleep, which you never seem able to manage
in bed. You told me, you know, that you
expected Cadman, that surly dirty fellow,
who delights to spoil my stones, and would
like nothing better than to take the pattern
out . of our drawing-room Kidderminster.
Now, I have a reason for saying something.
Charles, will you listen to me once, just
once ? "

"I never do anything else," said the
husband, with justice, and meaning no mischief.

"Ah ! how very seldom you hear me talk;
and when I do, I might just as well address
the winds ! But for once, my dear, attend,
I do implore you. That surly burly Cadman
will be here directly, and I know that you are
much put out with him. Now, I tell you, he
is dangerous, savagely dangerous ; I can see
it in his unhealthy skin. Oh, Charles, where
have you put down your pipe ? I cleaned that
shelf this very morning ! How little I thought
when I promised to be yours, that you ever
would knock out your ashes like that ! But

do bear in mind, dear, whatever you do, if anything happened to you, whatever would become of all of us ? All your sweet children, and your faithful wife—I declare you have made two great rings with your tumbler upon the new cover of the table."

"Matilda, that has been done ever so long. But I am almost certain this tumbler leaks."

"So you always say; just as if I would allow it. You never will think of simply wiping the rim every time you use it; when I put you a saucer for your glass, you forget it; there never was such a man, I do believe. I shall have to stop the rum and water altogether."

"No, no, no. I'll do anything you like. I'll have a tumbler made with a saucer to it —I'll buy a piece of oil-cloth the size of a fore-top sail—I'll—"

"Charles, no nonsense, if you please; as if I were ever unreasonable! But your quickness of temper is such, that I dread what you may say to that Cadman. Remember what opportunities he has, dear. He might shoot you in the dark any night, my darling, and put it upon the smugglers. I entreat you not to irritate the man, and make him your enemy. He is so spiteful; and I should be in terror the whole night long."

"Matilda, in the house you may command me as you please—even in my own cuddy here. But as regards my duty, you know well that I permit no interference. And I should have expected you to have more sense. A pretty officer I should be, if I were afraid of my own men. When a man is to blame, I tell him so, in good round language; and shall do so now. This man is greatly to blame, and I doubt whether to consider him a fool, or a rogue. If it were not that he has seven children, as we have, I would discharge him this very night."

"Charles, I am very sorry for his seven children; but our place is to think of our own seven first. I beg you, I implore you, to discharge the man; for he has not the courage to harm you, I believe, except with the cowardly advantage he has got. Now promise me either to say nothing to him, or to discharge him, and be done with him."

"Matilda, of such things you know nothing; and I cannot allow you to say any more."

"Very well, very well! I know my duty. I shall sit up and pray every dark night you are out, and the whole place will go to the dogs, of course. Of the smugglers I am not afraid one bit, nor of any honest fighting, such as you are used to. But oh, my dear Charles, the very bravest man can do nothing against base treachery."

"To dream of such things shows a bad imagination," Carroway answered sternly; but seeing his wife's eyes fill with tears, he took her hand gently, and begged her pardon, and promised to be very careful. "I am the last man to be rash," he said; "after getting so many more kicks than coppers. I never had a fellow under my command, who would lift a finger to harm me. And you must remember, my darling Tilly, that I command Englishmen, not Lascars."

With this she was forced to be content, to the best of her ability; and Geraldine ran bouncing in from school, to fill her father's pipe for him; so that by the time John Cadman came, his commander had almost forgotten the wrath created by the failure of the morning. But unluckily Cadman had not forgotten the words, and the look, he received before his comrades.

"Here I am, sir, to give an account of myself," he said in an insolent tone, having taken much liquor to brace him for the meeting. "Is it your pleasure to say out what you mean?"

"Yes, but not here. You will follow me to the station." The lieutenant took his favourite staff, and set forth; while his wife, from the little window, watched him with a very anxious gaze. She saw her husband stride in front, with the long rough gait she knew so well, and the swing of his arms which always showed that his temper was not in its best condition; and behind him Cadman slouched along, with his shoulders up, and his red hands clenched. And the poor wife sadly went back to work, for her life was a truly anxious one.

The station, as it was rather grandly called, was a hut about the size of a four-post bed, upon the low cliff, undermined by the sea, and even then threatened to be swept away. Here was a tall flag-staff for signals, and a place for a beacon-light when needed, and a bench with a rest for a spy-glass. In the hut itself were signal-flags, and a few spare muskets, and a keg of bullets, with maps and codes hung round the wall, and flint and tinder, and a

good many pipes, and odds and ends on
ledges. Carroway was very proud of this
place, and kept the key strictly in his own
pocket, and very seldom allowed a man to
pass through the narrow doorway. But he
liked to sit inside, and see them looking
desirous to come in.

"Stand there, Cadman," he said, as soon as
he had settled himself in the one hard chair;
and the man, though throughly primed for
revolt, obeyed the old habit, and stood outside.

"Once more you have misled me, Cadman,
and abused my confidence. More than that,
you have made me a common laughing-stock
for scores of fools, and even for a learned
gentleman, magistrate of divinity. I was
not content with your information, until you
confirmed it by letters you produced from
men well known to you, as you said, and
even from the inland trader, who had contracted for the venture. The schooner
'Elizabeth,' of Goole, disguised as a collier,
was to bring to, with Robin Lyth on board of
her, and the goods in her hold under cover-
ing of coal, and to run the goods at the
South Flamborough landing, this very night.

I have searched the 'Elizabeth' from stem to stern, and the craft brought up alongside of her; and all I have found is a wretched Frenchman, who skulked so that I made sure of him; and not a blessed anker of foreign brandy, nor even a 40 lb. bag of tea. You had that packet of letters in your neck-tie. Hand them to me this moment—"

"If your Honour has made up your mind to think that a sailor of the Royal Navy—"

"Cadman, none of that! No lick-spittle lies to me; those letters, that I may establish them! You shall have them back, if they are right. And I will pay you a half-crown for the loan."

"If I was to leave they letters in your hand, I could never hold head up in Burlington no more."

"That is no concern of mine. Your duty is to hold up your head with me, and those who find you in bread and butter."

"Precious little butter I ever gets, and very little bread to speak of. The folk that does the work gets nothing. Them that does nothing gets the name and game."

"Fellow, no reasoning, but obey me!" Carroway shouted, with his temper rising;

" hand over those letters, or you leave the service."

"How can I give away another man's property?" As he said these words, the man folded his arms, as who should say, "That is all you get out of me."

"Is that the way you speak to your commanding officer? Who owns those letters, then, according to your ideas?"

"Butcher Hewson; and he says that you shall have them, as soon as he sees the money for his little bill."

This was a trifle too much for Carroway. Up he jumped with surprising speed, took one stride through the station-door, and seizing Cadman by the collar, shook him, wrung his ear with the left hand, which was like a pair of pincers, and then with the other flung him backward, as if he were an empty bag. The fellow was too much amazed to strike, or close with him, or even swear, but received the vehement impact without any stay behind him. So that he staggered back, hat downward, and striking one heel on a stone, fell over the brink of the shallow cliff to the sand below.

The lieutenant, who never had thought of

this, was terribly scared, and his wrath turned cold. For although the fall was of no great depth, and the ground at the bottom so soft, if the poor man had struck it poll foremost, as he fell, it was likely that his neck was broken. Without any thought of his crippled heel, Carroway took the jump himself.

As soon as he recovered from the jar, which shook his stiff joints, and stiffer back, he ran to the coast-guardsman and raised him; and found him very much inclined to swear. This was a good sign, and the officer was thankful, and raised him in the gravelly sand, and kindly requested him to have it out, and to thank the Lord, as soon as he felt better. But Cadman, although he very soon came round, abstained from every token of gratitude. Falling with his mouth wide open in surprise, he had filled it with gravel of inferior taste, as a tidy sewer-pipe ran out just there, and at every execration he discharged a little.

"What can be done with a fellow so ungrateful?" cried the lieutenant, standing stiffly up again; "nothing but to let him come back to his manners. Hark you, John Cadman, between your bad words, if a glass of hot grog will restore your right wits, you can come up and have it, when your clothes are brushed."

With these words Carroway strode off to his cottage, without even deigning to look back; for a minute had been enough to show him that no very serious harm was done.

The other man did not stir, until his officer was out of sight; and then he arose, and rubbed himself, but did not care to go for his rummer of hot grog.

"I must work this off," the lieutenant said, as soon as he had told his wife, and received his scolding; "I cannot sit down; I must do something. My mind is becoming too much for me, I fear. Can you expect me to be laughed at? I shall take a little sail in the boat; the wind suits, and I have a particular reason. Expect me, my dear, when you see me."

In half-an-hour the largest boat, which carried a brass-swivel gun in her bows, was stretching gracefully across the bay, with her three white sails flashing back the sunset. The lieutenant steered, and he had four men with him, of whom Cadman was not one; that worthy being left at home to nurse his bruises and his dudgeon. These four men now were quite marvellously civil, having heard of their comrade's plight, and being pleased alike with that, and with their commander's prowess. For Cadman was by no means popular among them, because, though his pay was the same as theirs, he always tried to be looked up to; the while his manners were not distinguished, and scarcely could be called polite, when a supper required to be paid for. In derision of this, and of his desire for mastery, they had taken to call him " Boatswain Jack," or " John Boatswain," and provoked him by a subscription to present him with a pig-whistle. For these were men who liked well enough to receive hard words from their betters, who were masters of their business, but saw neither virtue nor value in submitting to superior airs from their equals.

The " Royal George," as this boat was called, passed through the fleet of quiet vessels, some of which trembled for a second visitation ; but not deigning to molest them she stood on, and rounding Flamborough Head, passed by the pillar rocks called King and Queen, and bore up for the North Landing cove. Here sail was taken in, and oars were manned; and Carroway ordered his men to pull in to the entrance of each of the well-known caves.

To enter these, when any swell is running, requires great care and experience; and the "Royal George" had too much beam to do it comfortably, even in the best of weather. And now, what the sailors call a "chopping sea" had set in with the turn of the tide, although the wind was still off-shore; so that even to lie-to at the mouth made rather a ticklish job of it. The men looked at one another, and did not like it, for a badly handled oar would have cast them on the rocks, which are villainously hard and jagged, and would stave in the toughest boat, like biscuit china. However, they durst not say that they feared it; and by skill and steadiness they examined all three caves quite enough to be certain that no boat was in them.

The largest of the three, and perhaps the finest, was the one they first came to, which already was beginning to be called the cave of Robin Lyth. The dome is very high, and sheds down light, when the gleam of the sea strikes inward. From the gloomy mouth of it, as far as they could venture, the lapping of the wavelets could be heard all round it, without a boat, or even a baulk of wood to break it. Then they tried echo, whose clear answer hesitates where any soft material is; but the shout rang only of hard rock and glassy water. To make assurance doubly sure, they lit a blue light and sent it floating through the depths, while they held their position with two boat-hooks and a fender. The cavern was lit up with a very fine effect, but not a soul inside of it to animate the scene. And to tell the truth, the bold invaders were by no means grieved at this; for if there had been smugglers there, it would have been hard to tackle them.

Hauling off safely, which was worse than running in, they pulled across the narrow cove, and rounding the little headland, examined the Church-cave and the Dovecot likewise, and with a like result. Then heartily tired, and well content with having done all that man could do, they set sail again in the dusk of the night, and forged their way against a strong ebb-tide towards the softer waters of Bridlington and the warmer comfort of their humble homes.

CHAPTER XVII.

DELICATE INQUIRIES.

A GENUINE summer day pays a visit nearly once in the season to Flamborough; and when it does come it has a wonderful effect. Often the sun shines brightly there, and often the air broods hot with thunder; but the sun owes his brightness to sweep of the wind, which sweeps away his warmth as well; while on the other hand, the thunder-clouds, like heavy smoke capping the headland, may oppress the air with heat, but are not of sweet summer's beauty.

For once, however, the fine day came, and the natives made haste to revile it. Before it was three hours old, they had found a hundred and fifty faults with it. Most of the men truly wanted a good sleep, after being lively all the night upon the waves,

and the heat and the yellow light came in
upon their eyes, and set the flies buzzing all
about them. And even the women, who had
slept out their time, and talked quietly, like
the clock ticking, were vexed with the sun,
which kept their kettles from good boiling,
and wrote upon their faces the years of their
life. But each made allowance for her
neighbour's appearance, on the strength of
the troubles she had been through.

For the matter of that, the sun cared not the
selvage of a shadow what was thought of
him, but went his bright way with a scattering of clouds and a tossing of vapours anywhere. Upon the few fishermen, who gave
up hope of sleep, and came to stand dazed
in their doorways, the glare of white walls
and chalky stones, and dusty roads, produced
the same effect as if they had put on their
father's goggles. Therefore they yawned
their way back to their room, and poked up
the fire, without which, at Flamborough, no
hot weather would be half hot enough.

The children, however, were wide awake,
and so were the washerwomen, whose turn
it had been to sleep last night for the labours
of the morning. These were plying hand

and tongue, in a little field by the three cross roads, where gaffers and gammers of bygone time had set up troughs of proven wood, and the bilge of a long storm-beaten boat, near a pool of softish water. Stout brown arms were roped with curd, and wedding-rings looked slippery things, and thumb-nails bordered with inveterate black, like broad beans ripe for planting, shone through a hubbub of snowy froth; while sluicing, and wringing, and rinsing went on, over the bubbled and lathery turf; and every handy bush or stub, and every tump of wiry grass was sheeted with white, like a ship in full sail, and shining in the sun-glare.

From time to time, these active women glanced back at their cottages, to see that the hearth was still alive, or at their little daughters squatting under the low wall which kept them from the road, where they had got all the babies to nurse, and their toes and other members to compare, and dandelion chains to make. But from their washing-ground, the women could not see the hill that brings to the bottom of the village the crooked road from Sewerby. Down that

hill came a horseman slowly, with nobody
to notice him, though himself on the watch
for everybody; and there in the bottom
below the first cottage, he allowed his horse
to turn aside, and cool hot feet and leathery
lips, in a brown pool spread by Providence
for the comfort of wayworn roadsters.

The horse looked as if he had laboured far,
while his rider was calmly resting; for the
cross-felled sutures of his flank were crusted
with grey perspiration, and the runnels of his
shoulders were dabbled; and now it behoved
him to be careful how he sucked the earthy-
flavoured water, so as to keep time with the
heaving of his barrel. In a word, he was
drinking as if he would burst—as his ostler
at home often told him—but the clever old
roadster knew better than that, and timing
it well between snorts and coughs was
tightening his girths with deep pleasure.

" Enough, my friend, is as good as a feast,"
said his rider to him gently, yet strongly pulling up the far-stretched head; " and too much
is worse than famine."

The horse, though he did not belong to
this gentleman, but was hired by him only
yesterday, had already discovered that, with

him on his back, his own judgment must lie dormant, so that he quietly whisked his tail and glanced with regret at the waste of his drip, and then, with a roundabout step, to prolong the pleasure of this little wade, sadly but steadily out he walked, and, after the necessary shake, began his first invasion of the village. His rider said nothing, but kept a sharp look-out.

Now this was Master Geoffrey Mordacks, of the ancient city of York, a general factor and land agent. What a " general factor" is, or is not, none but himself can pretend to say, even in these days of definition, and far less in times when thought was loose; and perhaps Mr. Mordacks would rather have it so. But any one who paid him well could trust him, according to the ancient state of things. To look at him, nobody would even dare to think that money could be a consideration to him, or the name of it other than an insult. So lofty and steadfast his whole appearance was, and he put back his shoulders so manfully. Upright, stiff, and well-appointed with a Roman nose, he rode with the seat of a soldier, and the decision of a tax-collector. From his long steel spurs to his hard coned hat not a soft line was there, nor a feeble curve. Stern honesty, and strict purpose stamped every open piece of him so strictly, that a man in a hedgerow fostering devious principles, and resolved to try them, could do no more than run away, and be thankful for the chance of it.

But in those rough and dangerous times, when thousands of people were starving, the view of a pistol-butt went further than sternest aspect of strong eyes. Geoffrey Mordacks well knew this, and did not neglect his knowledge. The brown walnut stock of a heavy pistol shone above either holster, and a cavalry sword in a leathern scabbard hung within easy reach of hand. Altogether this gentleman seemed not one to be rashly attacked by daylight.

No man had ever dreamed as yet of coming to this outlandish place for pleasure of the prospect. So that when this lonely rider was descried from the washing-field over the low wall of the lane, the women made up their minds at once that it must be a Justice of the Peace, or some great rider of the Revenue, on his way to see Dr. Upandown, or at the least a high constable concerned with some great sheep-stealing. Not that any such crime was known in the village itself of Flamborough, which confined its operations to the sea; but in the outer world of land that malady was rife just now, and a Flamborough man, too fond of mutton, had farmed some sheep on the downs, and lost them, which was considered a judgment on him for wilfully quitting ancestral ways.

But instead of turning at the corner where the rector was trying to grow some trees, the stranger kept on along the rugged highway, and between the straggling cottages, so that the women rinsed their arms, and turned round to take a good look at him, over the brambles and furze, and the wall of chalky flint and rubble.

"This is just what I wanted," thought Geoffrey Mordacks; "skill makes luck, and I am always lucky. Now, first of all, to recruit the inner man."

At this time Mrs. Theophila Precious, generally called "Tapsy," the widow of a man who had been lost at sea, kept the "Cod with a Hook in his Gills," the only hostelry in Flamborough village; although there was another towards the Landing. The cod had

been painted from life—or death—by a clever
old fisherman who understood him, and he
looked so firm, and stiff, and hard, that a
healthy man, with purse enough to tire of
butcher's meat, might grow in appetite by
gazing.   Mr. Mordacks pulled up and fixed
steadfast eyes upon this noble fish; the while
a score of sharp eyes from the green and white
meadow were fixed steadfastly on him.

"How he shines with salt water!   How
firm he looks, and his gills as bright as a rose
in June!   I have never yet tasted a cod at
first hand.   It is early in the day, but the air
is hungry. My expenses are paid, and I mean
to live well; for a strong mind will be required.
I will have a cut out of that fish, to begin
with."

Inditing of this, and of matters even better,
the rider turned into the yard of the inn,
where an old boat (as usual) stood for a horse-
trough, and sea-tubs served as buckets. Strong
sunshine glared upon the over-saling tiles,
and white buckled walls, and cracky lintels;
but nothing showed life, except an old yellow
cat, and a pair of house-martins who had
scarcely time to breathe, such a number of
little heads flipped out with a white flap under

the beak of each, demanding momentous
victualling. At these the yellow cat winked
with dreamy joyfulness, well aware how fat
they would be when they came to tumble
out.

"What a place of vile lazyness!" grumbled
Mr. Mordacks, as he got off his horse, after
vainly shouting "Hostler!" and led him to
the byre, which did duty for a stable. "York
is a lazy hole enough; but the further you go
from it the lazier they get. No energy, no
movement, no ambition anywhere. What a
country, what a people! I shall have to go
back and enlist the washerwomen."

A Yorkshireman might have answered this
complaint, if he thought it deserving of an
answer, by requesting Master Mordacks not
to be so over-quick, but to bide a wee bit
longer before he made so sure of the vast
superiority of his own wit, for the long heads
might prove better than the sharp ones in
the end of it. However, the general factor
thought that he could not have come to a
better place to get all that he wanted out of
everybody. He put away his saddle, and the
saddle-bags and sword, in a rough old sea-
chest with a padlock to it, and having a

sprinkle of chaff at the bottom. Then he
calmly took the key, as if the place were his,
gave his horse a rackful of long-cut grass,
and presented himself, with a lordly aspect,
at the front door of the silent inn. Here he
made noise enough to stir the dead; and at
the conclusion of a reasonable time, during
which she had finished a pleasant dream to
the simmering of the kitchen pot, the landlady showed herself in the distance, feeling
for her keys with one hand, and rubbing her
eyes with the other. This was the head-
woman of the village, but seldom tyrannical,
unless ill-treated, Widow Precious, tall and
square, and of no mean capacity.

" Young mon," with a deep voice she said,
" what is tha' deein' wi' aw that clatter?"

" Alas, my dear madam, I am not a young
man; and therefore time is more precious to
me. I have lived out half my allotted span,
and shall never complete it, unless I get
food."

" T' life o' mon is aw a hoory," replied
Widow Precious with slow truth. " Young
mon, what 'll ye hev?"

" Dinner, madam; dinner at the earliest
moment. I have ridden far, and my back

is sore, and my substance is calling for renewal."

"Ate, ate, ate, that's t' waa of aw menkins. Bud ye maa coom in, and crack o' it."

"Madam, you are most hospitable; and the place altogether seems to be of that description. What a beautiful room! May I sit down? I perceive a fine smell of most delicate soup. Ah, you know how to do things at Flamborough."

"Young mon, ye can ha' nune of yon potty. Yon's for mesell and t' childer."

"My excellent hostess, mistake me not. I do not aspire to such lofty pot-luck. I simply referred to it as a proof of your admirable culinary powers."

"Yon's beeg words. What 'll ye hev te ate?"

"A fish like that upon your sign-post, madam; or at least the upper half of him, and three dozen oysters just out of the sea, swimming in their own juice, with lovely melted butter."

"Young mon, hast tha' gotten t' brass? Them 'at ates offens forgets t' reck'nin'."

"Yes, madam, I have the needful in abundance. *Ecce signum!* Which is Latin, madam,

for the stamps of the king upon twenty
guineas. One to be deposited in your fair
hand for a taste, for a sniff, madam, such as
I had of your pot."

" Na, na. No tokkins till a' airned them.
What ood your Warship be for ating when a'
boileth ? "

The general factor, perceiving his way, was
steadfast to the shoulder-cut of a decent cod ;
and though the full season was scarcely yet
come, Mrs. Precious knew where to find one.
Oysters there were none, but she gave him
boiled limpets, and he thought it the manner
of the place that made them tough. After
these things he had a duck of the noblest and
best that live anywhere in England. Such
ducks were then, and perhaps are still, the
most remarkable residents of Flamborough.
Not only because the air is fine, and the pud-
dles and the dabblings of extraordinary merit,
and the wind fluffs up their pretty feathers
while alive, as the eloquent poulterer by-and-
by will do ; but because they have really distinguished birth, and adventurous, chivalrous,
and bright blue Norman blood. To such purpose do the gay young Vikings of the world of
quack pour in (when the weather and the time

of year invite), equipped with red boots and
plumes of purple velvet, to enchant the coy
lady ducks in soft water, and eclipse the
familiar and too legal drake. For a while
they revel in the change of scene, the luxury
of unsalted mud and scarcely rippled water,
and the sweetness and culture of tame dilly-
ducks, to whom their brilliant bravery, as well
as an air of romance and billowy peril com-
mend them too seductively. The responsible
sire of the pond is grieved, sinks his un-
appreciated bill into his back, and vainly
reflects upon the vanity of love.

From a loftier point of view, however, this
is a fine provision ; and Mr. Mordacks always
took a lofty view of everything.

"A beautiful duck, ma'am, a very grand
duck !" in his usual loud and masterful tone,
he exclaimed to Widow Precious. "I understand your question now as to my ability to
pay for him. Madam, he is worth a man's
last shilling. A goose is a smaller, and a
coarser bird. In what manner do you get
them ?"

"They gets their own sells, wi' the will of
the Lord. What will your Warship be for
ating, come after ?"

"None of your puddings and pies if you please, nor your excellent jellies and custards. A red Dutch cheese, with a pat of fresh butter, and another imperial pint of ale."

"Now yon is what I call a man," thought Mrs. Precious, having neither pie nor pudding, as Master Mordacks was well aware; "aisy to please, and a' knoweth what a' wants. A' mought a' been born i' Flaambro. A' maa baide for a week, if a' hath the tokens."

Mr. Mordacks felt that he had made his footing; but he was not the man to abide for a week, where a day would suit his purpose. His rule was never to beat about the bush when he could break through it, and he thought that he saw his way to do so now. Having finished his meal, he set down his knife with a bang, sat upright in the oaken' chair, and gazed in a bold yet pleasant manner at the sturdy hostess.

"You are wondering what has brought me here. That I will tell you in a very few words. Whatever I do is straightforward, madam; and all the world may know it. That has been my character throughout life; and in that respect I differ from the great bulk of mankind. You Flamborough folk, however,

are much of the very same nature as I am.
We ought to get on well together. Times
are very bad, very bad indeed. I could put
a good trifle of money in your way; but you
tell the truth without it, which is very, very
noble. Yet people with a family have duties
to discharge to them, and must sacrifice their
feelings to affection. Fifty guineas is a tidy
little figure, ma'am. With the famine growing in the land, no parent should turn his
honest back upon fifty guineas. And to get
the gold, and do good at the same time, is a
very rare chance indeed."

This speech was too much for Widow Precious to carry to her settled judgment, and
get verdict in a breath. She liked it, on the
whole, but yet there might be many things
upon the other side; so she did what Flamborough generally does, when desirous to
consider things, as it generally is. That is
to say, she stood with her feet well apart,
and her arms akimbo, and her head thrown
back to give the hinder part a rest, and no
sign of speculation in her eyes, although they
certainly were not dull. When these good
people are in this frame of mind and body, it
is hard to say whether they look more wise,

or foolish. Mr. Mordacks, impatient as he
was, even after so fine a dinner, was not far
from catching the infection of slow thought,
which spreads itself as pleasantly as that of
slow discourse.

"You are heeding me, madam; you have
quick wits," he said, without any sarcasm,
for she rescued the time from waste by afford-
ing a study of the deepest wisdom; "you are
wondering how the money is to come, and
whether it brings any risk with it. No,
Mistress Precious, not a particle of risk.
A little honest speaking is the one thing
needed."

"The money cometh scores of times, more
freely fra' wrong-doing."

"Your observation, madam, shows a deep
acquaintance with the human race. Too often
the money does come so; and thus it becomes
mere mammon. On such occasions we should
wash our hands, and not forget the charities.
But the beauty of money, fairly come by, is
that we can keep it all. To do good in
getting it, and do good with it, and to feel
ourselves better in every way, and our dear
children happier—this is the true way of considering the question. I saw some pretty

little dears peeping in, and wanted to give them a token or two, for I do love superior children. But you called them away, madam. You are too stern."

Widow Precious had plenty of sharp sense to tell her that her children were by no means "pretty dears" to anybody but herself, and to herself only when in a very soft state of mind; at other times they were but three gew-mouthed lasses, and two looby loons with teeth enough for crunching up the dripping-pan.

" Your Warship spaketh fair," she said; " a'most too fair, I'm doubting. Wad ye say what the maning is, and what name goeth pledge for the feefty poon, sir ?"

" Mistress Precious, my meaning always is plainer than a pikestaff; and as to pledges, the pledge is the hard cash down upon the nail, ma'am."

" Bank-tokkins, mayhap, and I prummeese to paa, with the sign of the Dragon, and a woman among sheeps."

" Madam, a bag of solid gold that can be weighed and counted. Fifty new guineas from the mint of King George, in a water-proof bag just fit to be buried at the foot of a

tree, or well under the thatch, or sewn up in
the sacking of your bedstead, ma'am. Ah,
pretty dreams, what pretty dreams, with a
virtuous knowledge of having done the right!
Shall we say it is a bargain, ma'am, and wet
it with a glass, at my expense, of the crystal
spring that comes under the sea?"

"Naw, sir, naw!—not till I knaw what. I
niver trafficks with the Divil, sir. There
wur a chap of Flaambro' deed—"

"My good madam, I cannot stop all day.
I have far to ride before nightfall. All
that I want is simply this, and having gone
so far I must tell you all, or make an enemy
of you. I want to match this; and I have
reason to believe that it can be matched in
Flamborough. Produce me the fellow, and
I pay you fifty guineas."

With these words Mr. Mordacks took from
an inner pocket a little pill-box, and thence
produced a globe, or rather an oblate spheroid
of bright gold, rather larger than a musket-
ball, but fluted or crenelled like a poppy-head,
and stamped or embossed with marks like
letters. Widow Precious looked down at it,
as if to think what an extraordinary thing it
was, but truly to hide from the stranger her

surprise at the sudden recognition. For Robin Lyth was a foremost favourite of hers, and most useful to her vocation; and neither fifty guineas nor five hundred should lead her to do him an injury. At a glance she had known that this bead must belong to the set from which Robin's ear-rings came; and perhaps it was her conscience which helped her to suspect that a trap was being laid for the free-trade hero. To recover herself, and have time to think, as well as for closer discretion, she invited Master Mordacks to the choice guest-chamber.

"Set ye doon, sir, hereaboot," she said, opening a solid door into the inner room; "neaver gain no fear at aw' o' crackin' o' the setties; fairm, fairm anoo' they be, thoo sketterish o' their lukes, sir. Set ye doon, your Warship; fafty poons desarveth a good room, wi'oot ony lugs o' anemees."

"What a beautiful room!" exclaimed Mr. Mordacks; "and how it savours of the place! I never should have thought of finding art and taste of such degree in a little place like Flamborough. Why, madam, you must have inherited it direct from the Danes themselves."

" Naw, sir, naw. I fetched it aw' oop fra'
the breck of the say and the cobbles. Book-
folk tooneth naw heed o' what we do."

" Well, it is worth a great deal of heed.
Lovely patterns of sea-weed on the floor, no
carpet can compare with them; shelves of—
I am sure I don't know what—fished up from
the deep no doubt; and shells innumerable,
and stones that glitter, and fish like glass,
and tufts like lace, and birds with most
wonderful things in their mouths; Mistress
Precious, you are too bad. The whole of it
ought to go to London, where they make
collections!"

" Lor, sir, how ye' da be laffin' at me. But
purty maa be said of 'em wi'out ony lees."

The landlady smiled as she set for him a
chair, towards which he trod gingerly and
picking every step, for his own sake as well
as of the garniture. For the black oak floor
was so oiled and polished, to set off the pattern of the sea-flowers on it (which really
were laid with no mean taste, and no small
sense of colour), that for slippery boots there
was some peril.

" This is a sacred as well as beautiful
place," said Mr. Mordacks. " I may finish

my words with safety here. Madam, I com-
mend your prudence as well as your excellent
skill and industry. I should like to bring
my daughter Arabella here; what a lesson she
would gain for tapestry! But now again,
for business. What do you say? Unless I
am mistaken, you have some knowledge of
the matter depending on this bauble. You
must not suppose that I came to you at
random. No, madam, no; I have heard far
away of your great intelligence, caution, and
skill, and influence in this important town.
'Mistress Precious, is the Mayor of Flamborough,' was said to me only last Saturday;
'if you would study the wise people there,
hang up your hat in her noble hostelry.'
Madam, I have taken that advice, and heartily
rejoice at doing so. I am a man of few
words, very few words—as you must have
seen already—but of the strictest straight-
forwardness in deeds. And now again, what
do you say, ma'am?"

"Your Warship hath left ma nowt to
saa. Your Warship hath had the mooth
aw to yosell."

"Now Mistress, Mistress Precious, truly
that is a little too bad of you. It is out of

my power to help admiring things which are
utterly beyond me to describe, and a dinner
of such cooking may enlarge the tongue,
after all the fine things it has been rolling in.
But business is my motto, in the fewest
words that may be. You know what I want;
you will keep it to yourself, otherwise other
people might demand the money. Through
very simple channels, you will find out
whether the fellow thing to this can be found
here, or elsewhere; and if so, who has got
it, and how it was come by, and everything
else that can be learned about it; and when
you know all, you just make a mark on this
piece of paper, ready folded, and addressed;
and then you will seal it, and give it to the
man who calls for the letters nearly twice a
week. And when I get that, I come and eat
another duck, and have oysters with my cod-
fish, which to-day we could not have, except
in the form of mussels, ma'am."

"Naw, not a moosel—they was aw' gude
flithers."

"Well, ma'am, they may have been unknown animals; but good they were, and as
fresh as the day. Now, you will remember
that my desire is to do good. I have nothing

to do with the revenue, nor the magistrates, nor his Majesty. I shall not even go to your parson, who is the chief authority, I am told; for I wish this matter to be kept quiet, and beside the law altogether. The whole credit of it shall belong to you, and a truly good action you will have performed, and done a little good for your own good self. As for this trinket, I do not leave it with you, but I leave you this model in wax, ma'am, made by my daughter, who is very clever. From this you can judge quite as well as from the other. If there are any more of these things in Flamborough, as I have strong reason to believe, you will know best where to find them, and I need not tell you that they are almost certain to be in the possession of a woman. You know all the women, and you skilfully inquire, without even letting them suspect it. Now, I shall just stretch my legs a little, and look at your noble prospect, and in three hours' time a little more refreshment, and then, Mistress Precious, you see the last of your obedient servant, until you demand from him fifty gold guineas."

After seeing to his horse again, he set forth for a stroll, in the course of which he met with Dr. Upround and his daughter. The rector looked hard at this distinguished stranger, as if he desired to know his name, and expected to be accosted by him, while quick Miss Janetta glanced with undisguised suspicion, and asked her father, so that Mr. Mordacks overheard it, what business such a man could have, and what could he come spying after, in their quiet parish? The general factor raised his hat, and passed on with a tranquil smile, taking the crooked path which leads along and around the cliffs, by way of the light-house, from the north to the southern landing. The present light-house was not yet built; but an old round tower, which still exists, had long been used as a signal-station, for semaphore by day, and at night for beacon, in the times of war and tumult; and most people called it the "Monument." This station was now of very small importance, and sometimes did nothing for a year together; but still it was very good and useful, because it enabled an ancient tar, whose feet had been carried away by a cannon-ball, to draw a little money once a month, and to think himself still a fine British bulwark.

In the summer-time, this hero always
slung his hammock here, with plenty of wind
to rock him off to sleep; but in winter King
Æolus himself could not have borne it.
" Monument Joe," as almost everybody called
him, was a queer old character of days gone
by. Sturdy and silent, but as honest as the
sun, he made his rounds as regularly as that
great orb, and with equally beneficent object.
For twice a day he stumped to fetch his beer
from Widow Precious, and the third time to
get his little panniken of grog. And now
the time was growing for that last important
duty, when a stranger stood before him with
a crown-piece in his hand.

" Now don't get up, captain, don't disturb
yourself," said Mr. Mordacks graciously;
" your country has claimed your activity, I see,
and I hope it makes amends to you. At the
same time, I know that it very seldom does.
Accept this little tribute from the admiration
of a friend."

Old Joe took the silver piece and rang it
on his tin tobacco-box, then stowed it inside,
and said, " Gammon! What d'ye want of
me ? "

" Your manners, my good sir, are scarcely

on a par with your merits. I bribe no man;
it is the last thing I would ever dream of
doing. But whenever a question of memory
arises, I have often observed a great failure
of that power, without—without, if you will
excuse the expression, the administration of
a little grease."

"Smooggling? Aught about smooggling?"
Old Joe shut his mouth sternly; for he
hated and scorned the coast-guards, whose
wages were shamefully above his own, and
who had the impudence to order him for
signals; while on the other hand he found
free-trade a policy liberal, enlightening, and
inspiriting.

"No, captain, no; not a syllable of that.
You have been in this place about sixteen
years. If you had only been here four years
more, your evidence would have settled all
I want to know. No wreck can take place
here, of course, without your knowledge?"

"Dunno that. B'lieve one have. There's
a twist of the tide here—but what good to
tell landlubbers?"

"You are right. I should never understand such things. But I find them wonderfully interesting. You are not a native of

this place, and knew nothing of Flamborough before you came here?"

Monument Joe gave a grunt at this, and a long squirt of tobacco-juice. "And don't want," he said.

"Of course, you are superior, in every way superior. You find these people rough, and far inferior in manners. But either, my good friend, you will reopen your tobacco-box, or else you will answer me a few short questions, which trespass in no way upon your duty to the king, or to his loyal smugglers."

Old Joe looked up, with weather-beaten eyes, and saw that he had no fool to deal with, in spite of all soft palaver. The intensity of Mr. Mordacks' eyes made him blink, and mutter a bad word or two, but remain pretty much at his service. And the last intention he could entertain was that of restoring this fine crown-piece. "Spake on, sir," he said; "and I will spake accordin'."

"Very good. I shall give you very little trouble. I wish to know whether there was any wreck here, kept quiet perhaps, but still some ship lost, about three or four years before you came to this station. It does not

matter what ship, any ship at all, which may
have gone down without any fuss at all.
You know of none such? Very well. You
were not here; and the people of this place
are wonderfully close. But a veteran of the
Royal Navy should know how to deal with
them. Make your inquiries, without seeming
to inquire. The question is altogether private,
and cannot in any way bring you into
trouble. Whereas, if you find out anything,
you will be a made man, and live like a
gentleman. You hate the lawyers? All the
honest seamen do. I am not a lawyer; and
my object is to fire a broadside into them.
Accept this guinea; and if it would suit you
to have a crown every week for the rest of your
life, I will pledge you my word for it, paid
in advance, if you only find out for me one
little fact, of which I have no doubt whatever, that a merchant ship was cast away
near this Head, just about nineteen years
agone."

That ancient sailor was accustomed to
surprises; but this, as he said, when he came
to think of it, made a clean sweep of him,
fore and aft. Nevertheless he had the
presence of mind required for pocketing the

guinea, which was too good for his tobacco-
box; and as one thing at a time was quite
enough upon his mind, he probed away slowly,
to be sure there was no hole. Then he got
up from his squatting form, with the usual
activity of those who are supposed to have
none left, and touched his brown hat, standing cleverly. "What be I to do for all this?"
he asked.

"Nothing more than what I have told you.
To find out slowly, and without saying why,
in the way you sailors know how to do,
whether such a thing came to pass, as I
suppose. You must not be stopped by the
lies of anybody. Of course they will deny it,
if they got some of the wrecking; or it is
just possible that no one even heard of it;
and yet there may be some traces. Put two
and two together, my good friend, as you
have the very best chance of doing; and
soon you may put two to that in your pocket,
and twenty, and a hundred, and as much as
you can hold."

"When shall I see your good Honour
again, to score log-run, and come to a
reckoning?"

"Master Joseph, work a wary course.

Your rating for life will depend upon that. You may come to this address, if you have anything important. Otherwise you shall soon hear of me again. Good-bye."

CHAPTER XVIII.

GOYLE BAY.

WHILE all the world was at cross-purposes thus,—Mr. Jellicorse uneasy at some rumours he had heard; Captain Carroway splitting his poor heel with indignation at the craftiness of free-traders; Farmer Anerley vexed at being put upon by people, without any daughter to console him, or catch shrimps; Master Mordacks pursuing a noble game, strictly above board, as usual; Robin Lyth, troubled in his largest principles of revolt against revenue, by a nasty little pain that kept going to his heart, with an emptiness there, as for another heart; and last, and perhaps of all most important, the rector perpetually pining for his game of chess, and utterly discontented with the frigid embraces of analysis—where was the best, and most

simple, and least selfish of the whole lot,
Mary Anerley?

Mary was in as good a place as even she
was worthy of. A place not by any means
so snug and favoured by nature as Anerley
Farm, but pretty well sheltered by large trees
of a strong and hardy order. And the
comfortable ways of good old folk, who
needed no labour to live by, spread a happy
leisure, and a gentle ease, upon everything
under their roof-tree. Here was no necessity
for getting up, until the sun encouraged it;
and the time for going to bed depended upon
the time of sleepiness. Old Johnny Popplewell,
as everybody called him, without any protest
on his part, had made a good pocket by the
tanning business, and having no children to
bring up to it, and only his wife to depend
upon him, had sold the good-will, the yard,
and the stock, as soon as he had turned his
sixtieth year. "I have worked hard all my
life," he said; "and I mean to rest for the
rest of it."

At first he was heartily miserable, and
wandered about with a vacant look, having
only himself to look after. And he tried to
find a hole in his bargain with the man who

enjoyed all the smells he was accustomed to,
and might even be heard through a gap in
the fence, rating the men as old Johnny used
to do, at the same time of day, and for the
same neglect, and almost in the self-same
words which the old owner used, but stronger.
Instead of being happy, Master Popplewell
lost more flesh in a month than he used to
lay on in the most prosperous year; and he
owed it to his wife, no doubt, as generally
happens, that he was not speedily gathered
to the bosom of the hospitable Simon of
Joppa. For Mrs. Popplewell said, "Go
away; Johnny, go away from this village;
smell new smells, and never see a hide without a walking thing inside of it. Sea-weed
smells almost as nice as tan; though of course
it is not so wholesome." The tanner obeyed,
and bought a snug little place about ten
miles from the old premises, which he called,
at the suggestion of the parson, "Byrsa
Cottage."

Here was Mary, as blithe as a lark, and as
petted as a robin red-breast, by no means
pining, or even hankering, for any other robin.
She was not the girl to give her heart before
it was even asked for; and hitherto she had

regarded the smuggler with pity more than
admiration.   For in many points she was
like her father, whom she loved foremost of
the world; and Master Anerley was a law-
abiding man, like every other true English-
man.   Her uncle Popplewell was also such,
but exerted his principles less strictly.   Moreover, he was greatly under influence of wife,
which happens more freely to. a man without
children, the which are a source of contradiction.   And Mistress Popplewell was a
most thorough and conscientious free-trader.

Now Mary was from childhood so accustomed to the sea, and the relish of salt
breezes, and the racy dance of little waves
that crowd on one another, and the tidal
delivery of delightful rubbish, that to fail
of seeing the many works and plays, and
constant variance of her never wearying or
weary friend, was more than she could long
put up with.   She called upon 'Lord Keppel'
almost every day, having brought him from
home for the good of his health, to gird up
his loins, or rather get his belly-girths on,
and come along the sands with her, and dig
into new places.   But he, though delighted
for a while with Byrsa stable, and the social

charms of Master Popplewell's old cob, and a
rick of fine tan-coloured clover-hay and bean-
haulm—when the novelty of these delights
was passed, he pined for his home, and the
split in his crib, and the knot of hard wood
he had polished with his neck, and even the
little dog that snapped at him. He did not
care for retired people—as he said to the cob
every evening—he liked to see farm-work
going on, or at any rate to hear all about it,
and to listen to horses who had worked hard,
and could scarcely speak for chewing, about
the great quantity they had turned of earth,
and how they had answered very bad words
with a bow. In short, to put it in the mildest
terms, Lord Keppel was giving himself great
airs, unworthy of his age, ungrateful to a
degree, and ungraceful, as the cob said
repeatedly; considering how he was fed, and
bedded, and not a thing left undone for him.
But his arrogance soon had to pay its own
costs.

For, away to the right of Byrsa Cottage,
as you look down the hollow of the ground
towards the sea, a ridge of high scrubby
land runs up to a fore-front of bold cliff,
indented with a dark and narrow bay.

"Goyle Bay" as it is called, or sometimes "Basin Bay," is a lonely and rugged place, and even dangerous for unwary visitors. For at low spring tides a deep hollow is left dry, rather more than a quarter of a mile across, strewn with kelp and oozy stones, among which may often be found pretty shells, weeds richly tinted and of subtle workmanship, stars, and flowers, and love-knots of the sea, and sometimes carnelions and crystals. But anybody making a collection here should be able to keep one eye upward and one down, or else in his pocket to have two things—a good watch and a trusty tide-table.

John and Deborah Popplewell were accustomed to water in small supplies, such as that of a well, or a roadside pond, or their own old noble tan-pits; but to understand the sea it was too late in life, though it pleased them and gave them fine appetites now, to go down when it was perfectly calm, and a sailor assured them that the tide was mild. But even at such seasons they preferred to keep their distance, and called out frequently to one another. They looked upon their niece from all she told them, as a creature

almost amphibious; but still they were often
uneasy about her, and would gladly have
kept her well inland; she, however, laughed
at any such idea; and their discipline was to
let her have her own way. But now a thing
happened which proved for ever how much
better old heads are than young ones.

For Mary, being tired of the quiet places,
and the strands where she knew every pebble,
resolved to explore Goyle Bay at last, and
she chose the worst possible time for it. The
weather had been very fine and gentle, and
the sea delightfully plausible, without a
wave—tide after tide—bigger than the
furrow of a two-horse plough; and the maid
began to believe at last that there never
were any storms just here. She had heard
of the pretty things in Goyle Bay, which
was difficult of access from the land, but
she resolved to take opportunity of tide,
and thus circumvent the position; she would
rather have done it afoot, but her uncle
and aunt made a point of her riding to the
shore, regarding the pony as a safe com-
panion, and sure refuge from the waves.
And so, upon the morning of St. Michael,
she compelled Lord Keppel, with an adverse

mind, to turn a headland they had never turned before.

The tide was far out and ebbing still, but the wind had shifted and was blowing from the east rather stiffly, and with increasing force. Mary knew that the strong equinoctial tides were running at their height; but she had timed her visit carefully, as she thought, with no less than an hour and a half to spare. And even without any thought of tide, she was bound to be back in less time than that, for her uncle had been most particular to warn her to be home without fail at one o'clock, when the sacred goose, to which he always paid his duties, would be on the table. And if anything marred his serenity of mind, it was to have dinner kept waiting.

Without any misgivings, she rode into Basin Bay, keeping within the black barrier of rocks, outside of which wet sands were shining. She saw that these rocks, like the bar of a river, crossed the inlet of the cove; but she had not been told of their peculiar frame and upshot, which made them so treacherous a rampart. At the mouth of the bay they formed a level crescent, as even as a set of good teeth, against the sea, with a slope of sand running up to their outer front, but a deep and long pit inside of them. This pit drained itself very nearly dry when the sea went away from it, through some stony tubes which only worked one way, by the closure of their mouths when the tide returned; so that the volume of the deep sometimes, with tide and wind behind it, leaped over the brim into the pit, with tenfold the roar, a thousand-fold the power, and scarcely less than the speed of a lion.

Mary Anerley thought what a lovely place it was, so deep and secluded from anybody's sight, and full of bright wet colours. Her pony refused, with his usual wisdom, to be dragged to the bottom of the hole, but she made him come further down than he thought just, and pegged him by the bridle there. He looked at her sadly, and with half a mind to expostulate more forcibly, but getting no glimpse of the sea where he stood, he thought it as well to put up with it; and presently he snorted out a tribe of little creatures, which puzzled him and took up his attention.

Meanwhile, Mary was not only puzzled, but delighted beyond description. She never yet had come upon such treasures of the sea, and she scarcely knew what to lay hands upon first. She wanted the weeds of such wonderful forms, and colours yet more exquisite, and she wanted the shells of such delicate fabric, that fairies must have made them, and a thousand other little things that had no names; and then she seemed most of all to want the pebbles. For the light came through them in stripes and patterns, and many of them looked like downright jewels. She had brought a great bag of strong canvas luckily, and with both hands she set to, to fill it.

So busy was the girl with the vast delight of sanguine acquisition—this for her father, and that for her mother, and so much for everybody she could think of—that time had no time to be counted at all, but flew by with feathers unheeded. The mutter of the sea became a roar, and the breeze waxed into a heavy gale, and spray began to sputter through the air, like suds; but Mary saw the rampart of the rocks before her, and thought that she could easily get back around the point. And her taste began continually to grow more choice, so that she spent as much time in discarding the rubbish which at first she had prized so highly, as she did in collecting the real rarities, which she was learning to distinguish. But unluckily, the sea made no allowance for all this.

For just as Mary, with her bag quite full, was stooping with a long stretch to get something more—a thing that perhaps was the very best of all, and therefore had got into a corner, there fell upon her back quite a solid lump of wave, as a horse gets the bottom of the bucket cast at him. This made her look up, not a minute too soon; and even then she was not at all aware of danger, but took it for a notice to be moving. And she thought more of shaking that salt water from her dress, than of running away from the rest of it.

But as soon as she began to look about in earnest, sweeping back her salted hair, she saw enough of peril to turn pale the roses, and strike away the smile upon her very busy face. She was standing several yards below the level of the sea, and great surges were hurrying to swallow her. The hollow of the rocks received the first billow with a thump and a slush, and a rush of pointed hillocks in a fury to find their way back again; which failing, they spread into a long white pool, taking Mary above her pretty ankles. "Don't you think to frighten me," said Mary; " I know all your ways, and I mean to take my time."

But even before she had finished her words, a great black wall (doubled over at the top with whiteness, that seemed to race along it like a fringe) hung above the rampart, and leaped over, casting at Mary such a volley that she fell. This quenched her last audacity, although she was not hurt; and jumping up nimbly she made all haste through the rising water towards her pony. But as she would not forsake her bag, and the rocks became more and more slippery, towering higher and higher surges crashed in over the barrier, and swelled the yeasty turmoil which began to fill the basin; while a scurry of foam flew, like pellets from the rampart, blinding even the very best young eyes.

Mary began to lose some of her presence of mind, and familiar approval of the sea. She could swim pretty well from her frequent bathing; but swimming would be of little service here, if once the great rollers came over the bar, which they threatened to do every moment. And when at length she fought her way to the poor old pony, her danger and distress were multiplied. Lord Keppel was in a state of abject fear; despair was knocking at his fine old heart; he was up to his knees in the loathsome brine already, and being so twisted up by his own exertions, that to budge another inch was beyond him, he did what a horse is apt to do in such condition, he consoled himself with fatalism. He meant to expire; but before he did so, he determined to make his mistress feel what she had done. Therefore, with a sad nudge of white old nose, he drew her attention to his last expression, sighed as plainly as a man could sigh, and fixed upon her meek eyes, telling volumes.

"I know, I know that it is all my fault," cried Mary, with the brine almost smothering her tears, as she flung her arms around his neck; "but I never will do it again, my darling. And I never will run away and let you drown. Oh, if I only had a knife! I cannot even cast your bridle off; the tongue has stuck fast, and my hands are cramped. But, Keppel, I will stay, and be drowned with you."

This resolve was quite unworthy of Mary's common sense; for how could her being drowned with Keppel help him? However, the mere conception showed a spirit of lofty order; though the body might object to be ordered under. Without any thought of all that, she stood, resolute, tearful, aad thoroughly wet through, while she hunted in her pocket for a penknife.

The nature of all knives is, not to be found; and Mary's knife was loyal to its kind. Then she tugged at her pony, and pulled out his bit, and laboured again at the obstinate strap; but nothing could be done with it. Keppel must be drowned, and he did not seem to care, but to think that the object of his birth was that. If the stupid little fellow would have only stepped forward, the hands of his mistress, though cramped and benumbed, might perhaps have unbuckled his stiff and sodden reins, or even undone their tangle; on the other hand, if he would have jerked with all his might, something or other must have given way; but stir he would not from one fatuous position, which kept all his headgear on the strain, but could not snap it. Mary even struck him with her heavy bag of

stones, to make him do something; but he
only looked reproachful.

"Was there ever such a stupid?" the poor
girl cried, with the water rising almost to her
waist, and the inner waves beginning to dash
over her, while the outer billows threatened to
rush in and crush them both. "But I will not
abuse you any more, poor Keppel. What will
dear father say? Oh, what will he think of it?"

Then she burst into a fit of sobs, and leaned
against the pony, to support her from a rushing wave which took her breath away, and
she thought that she would never try to
look up any more, but shut her eyes to all the
rest of it. But suddenly she heard a loud
shout and a splash, and found herself caught
up and carried like an infant.

"Lie still. Never mind the pony; what is
he? I will go for him afterwards. You first,
you first of all the world, my Mary."

She tried to speak, but not a word would
come; and that was all the better. She was
carried quick as might be through a whirl of
tossing waters, and gently laid upon a pile of
kelp; and then Robin Lyth said, "You are
quite safe here, for at least another hour. I
will go and get your pony."

"No, no; you will be knocked to pieces," she cried; for the pony, in the drift and scud, could scarcely be seen but for his helpless struggles. But the young man was halfway towards him while she spoke, and she knelt upon the kelp, and clasped her hands.

Now Robin was at home in a matter such as this. He had landed many kegs in a sea as strong or stronger, and he knew how to deal with the horses in a surf. There still was a break of almost a fathom in the level of the inner and the outer waves, for the basin was so large that it could not fill at once; and so long as this lasted, every roller must comb over at the entrance, and mainly spend itself. "At least five minutes to spare," he shouted back, "and there is no such thing as any danger." But the girl did not believe him.

Rapidly and skilfully he made his way, meeting the larger waves sideways and rising at their onset; until he was obliged to swim at last where the little horse was swimming desperately. The leather, still jammed in some crevice at the bottom, was jerking his poor chin downwards; his eyes were screwed up like a new-born kitten's, and his dainty nose looked like a jelly-fish. He thought how sad it was that he should ever die like this, after all the good works of his life—the people he had carried, and the chaise that he had drawn, and all his kindness to mankind. Then he turned his head away, to receive the stroke of grace, which the next wave would administer.

No! He was free. He could turn his honest tail on the sea, which he always had detested so; he could toss up his nose and blow the filthy salt out, and sputter back his scorn, while he made off for his life. So intent was he on this, that he never looked twice, to make out who his benefactor was, but gave him just a taste of his hind-foot on the elbow, in the scuffle of his hurry to be round about and off. "Such is gratitude!" the smuggler cried, but a clot of salt water flipped into · his mouth, and closed all cynical outlet. Bearing up against the waves he stowed his long knife away, and then struck off for the shore with might and main.

Here Mary ran into the water to meet him, shivering as she was with fright and cold, and stretched out both hands to him, as he waded forth; and he took them and clasped them, quite as if he needed help. Lord Keppel

stood afar off, recovering his breath, and
scarcely dared to look askance at the exe-
crable sea.

"How cold you are!" Robin Lyth exclaimed. "You must not stay a moment.
No talking if you please—though I love your
voice so. You are not safe yet. You cannot get
back round the point. See the waves dashing
up against it! You must climb the cliff, and
that is no easy job for a lady, in the best of
weather. In a couple of hours, the tide will
be over the whole of this beach a fathom
deep. There is no boat nearer than Filey;
and a boat could scarcely live over that bar.
You must climb the cliff, and begin at once,
before you get any colder."

"Then is my poor pony to be drowned
after all? If he is, he had better have been
drowned at once."

The smuggler looked at her with a smile,
which meant, "Your gratitude is about the
same as his;" but he answered, to assure
her, though by no means sure himself,—

"There is time enough for him; he shall
not be drowned. But you must be got out of
danger first. When you are off my mind, I
will fetch up pony. Now you must follow

me step by step, carefully and steadily. I
would carry you up, if I could; but even a
giant could scarcely do that, in a stiff gale of
wind, and with the crag so wet."

Mary looked up with a shiver of dismay.
She was brave and nimble, generally, but now
so wet and cold, and the steep cliff looked so
slippery, that she said, " It is useless; I can
never get up there. Captain Lyth, save yourself, and leave me."

" That would be a pretty thing to do," he
replied; " and where should I be afterwards ?
I am not at the end of my devices yet. I
have got a very snug little crane up there. It
was here we ran our last lot, and beat the
brave lieutenant so. But unluckily I have no
cave just here. None of my lads are about
here now, or we would make short work of it.
But I could hoist you very well, if you would
let me."

" I would never think of such a thing. To
come up like a keg! Captain Lyth, you
must know that I never would be so dis-
graced."

" Well, I was afraid that you might take it
so ; though I cannot see why it should be any
harm. We often hoist the last man so."

"It is different with me," said Mary; "it may be no harm; but I could not have it."

The free-trader looked at her bright eyes and colour, and admired her spirit which his words had roused.

"I pray your forgiveness, Miss Anerley," he said, "I meant no harm. I was thinking of your life. But you look now as if you could do anything almost."

"Yes, I am warm again. I have no fear. I will not go up like a keg, but like myself. I can do it without help from anybody."

"Only please to take care not to cut your little hands," said Robin as he began the climb; for he saw that her spirit was up to do it.

"My hands are not little; and I will cut them if I choose. Please not even to look back at me. I am not in the least afraid of anything."

The cliff was not of the soft and friable stuff to be found at Bridlington, but of hard and slippery sandstone, with bulky ribs oversaling here and there, and threatening to cast the climber back. At such spots, nicks for the feet had been cut, or broken with a hammer, but scarcely wider than a stirrup-iron, and far less inviting. To surmount these was quite impossible, except by a process of crawling; and Mary, with her heart in her mouth, repented of her rash contempt for the crane-sling. Luckily the height was not very great, or, tired as she was, she must have given way; for her bodily warmth had waned again in the strong wind buffeting the cliff. Otherwise the wind had helped her greatly by keeping her from swaying outward; but her courage began to fail at last, and very near the top she called for help. A short piece of lanyard was thrown to her at once, and Robin Lyth landed her on the bluff, panting, breathless, and blushing again.

"Well done!" he cried, gazing as she turned her face away; "young ladies may teach even sailors to climb. Not every sailor could get up this cliff. Now, back to Master Popplewell's as fast as you can run, and your Aunt will know what to do with you."

"You seem well acquainted with my family affairs," said Mary, who could not help smiling. "Pray, how did you even know where I am staying?"

"Little birds tell me everything; especially

about the best, and most gentle, and beautiful of all birds."

The maiden was inclined to be vexed again; but remembering how much he had done, and how little gratitude she had shown, she forgave him, and asked him to come to the cottage.

"I will bring up the little horse. Have no fear," he replied; "I will not come up at all unless I bring him. But it may take two or three hours."

With no more than a waive of his hat, he set off, as if the Coast-riders were after him, by the path along the cliffs towards Filey, for he knew that Lord Keppel must be hoisted by the crane, and he could not manage it without another man; and the tide would wait for none of them. Upon the next headland he found one of his men, for the smugglers maintained a much sharper look-out than did the forces of his Majesty, because they were paid much better; and returning they managed to strap Lord Keppel, and hoist him like a big bale of contraband goods. For their crane had been left in a brambled hole; and they very soon rigged it out again. The little horse kicked pretty freely in the air, not perceiving his own welfare; but a cross-beam and pulley kept him well out from the cliff, and they swung him in over handsomely, and landed him well upon the sward within the brink. Then they gave him three cheers for his great adventure, which he scarcely seemed to appreciate.

END OF VOL. I.

LONDON :
GILBERT AND RIVINGTON, PRINTERS,
ST. JOHN'S SQUARE.